To Rya

The MYSTERY of the

SCIENCE TEACHER

Read on!

The **MYSTERY** of the

SCIENCE TEACHER

Marty Chan

thistledown press

Library and Archives Canada Cataloguing in Publication

Chan, Marty
The mystery of the mad science teacher / Marty Chan.
ISBN 978-1-897235-38-6
I. Title.
PS8555.H39244M984 2008   jC813'.54   C2008-900075-7

Cover illustration by Laura Lee Osborne
Cover and book design by Jackie Forrie

Thistledown Press Ltd.
410 2nd Avenue North
Saskatoon, Saskatchewan, S7K 2C3
www.thistledownpress.com

We acknowledge the support of the Canada Council for the Arts, the Saskatchewan Arts Board, and the Government of Canada for our publishing program.

ACKNOWLEDGEMENTS

Diane Tucker, Cheryl Hoover, Wei Wong, Michelle Chan, Laura Lee Osborne, Dovercourt School, Grovenor School, St. Timothy School, Ann Blakely, Julie Johnson, Anna Perri, and the Alberta Foundation for the Arts.

ONE

The two things a guy can never take back are the oversized baby blue sweater his aunt gives him for his birthday — and the promise he makes to a friend.

Right about now I wished I had the itchy sweater Big Auntie gave me last year, because I needed it to protect me from my promise to Remi Boudreau. I told my best friend I'd help him with slapshot practice. Little did I know this meant I had to stand in net while pucks flew at me like angry hornets. I reminded myself that Remi wanted to get the puck past me, but I also knew that the goal counted if the puck went *through* me.

If I'd had real goalie pads, I wouldn't have been so worried, but I couldn't afford hockey equipment. Remi loaned me his helmet, but the rest of my gear came from my parents' grocery store. I stuffed U.F.O.

magazines into my knee-high athletic socks. The edges of the magazines dug into the tops of my feet and left temporary tattoos of smudgy alien faces on my shins. Still, they gave me more protection than my short-sleeved T-shirt or my oven mitt hockey gloves. Remi's slap shots created the kind of heat even the oven mitts couldn't handle. Instead of catching the pucks, I tried to bat the blistering biscuits out of the air with the fly swatter I used as my goalie stick. I felt more like a sitting duck than a goaltender.

"You ready, Marty?" Remi yelled from the other end of the street.

"Another minute," I squeaked. More like another year.

He stick-handled the puck and worked himself into position about fifty feet from the net, but from where I stood it looked more like he was right in front of me. He wound up. My face shield fogged up from my panting breath and wiped out my vision. I rubbed the outside of the shield with my oven mitt until I realized the fog was on the inside. I couldn't see anything. In that horrible moment before the shot, I realized I'd forgotten to protect the most important part of my body. Where was my jockstrap and cup? Too late. *Ker-rack!*

"He shoots! He scores!" Remi yelled.

I breathed a sigh of relief and flipped up my face shield. The maple leaf on Remi's blue and white hockey jersey flapped in the breeze as he lunged forward and speared the air with his stick. Behind the pop can goalposts, about halfway down the street, the puck rolled to a stop and fell over.

"Good shot, Remi," I said.

"I could have snuck a dump truck past you," he teased. "Move the posts closer together so it's harder to score."

"Um, do you have a cup?" I asked.

"Why? Are you thirsty?"

"No. For my... You know."

He scratched his head. Then he realized what I wanted. "Oh. Just stick one of the magazines down your pants."

The magazine was already killing my feet. I could only imagine what it'd do to the other bits of my body.

"Get the puck and let's go," Remi barked.

Every inch of my tender skin screamed "run away," but I couldn't let my pal down. I recovered the puck.

"Hurry up, Chan." He used my last name whenever he wanted to play serious hockey.

I shambled back to the net and rolled the puck to my pal. Then I stepped between the pop can goalposts, squeezed my legs together and imagined very thin things: *sign post, a pencil, kite string* . . . My face shield fogged up again. I waited for the loud crack, but nothing happened. Instead, a bicycle bell rang from somewhere behind me.

"Car!" yelled a girl's voice.

The best word in the entire English language! "Car" was better than "Christmas present," "video game" and "bacon-rolled shrimp" crammed into one super word. I opened my eyes. A gold Cadillac had stopped behind Remi. He kicked the puck off the road and stepped aside. I grabbed the pop cans and walked to the grassy curb.

Once we were clear, the car lurched forward. The oldest driver in the world, Mrs. Johnson, gripped the top of the steering wheel, her head barely high enough to see the road. Her golden slug-mobile stutter-rolled past me. Halfway down the street, balanced on her mountain bike, Trina Brewster waved at us.

Once my mortal enemy, Trina was now sort of a friend, but not the way Remi was a friend. The only time she'd hang out with me was when she said her other pals were busy and she was bored. I was like the armless doll she kept in the bottom of her toy box and brought out only after she'd lost her cool toys.

She climbed off her black bike and took off her red helmet. Over the summer holidays Trina's long hair had turned sunflower yellow. She was also a few inches taller. Most important of all, Trina's semi-permanent sneer — the one she usually showed me and no one else — had been replaced with a smile that drew my eyes to her face like a kitten to a sunbeam.

"Did you miss me?" she asked.

Remi's mouth hung open, but he didn't say a word. He stared, his eyes wide with kitten wonder. I wasn't the only one who had noticed the change in Trina.

"You look different," I said.

"Different?" Her smile dropped.

"Good. He meant good," Remi said, jumping to my defence.

I nodded. Her warm smile returned. My kitten head bobbed up and down in silent approval.

"Do you want to watch me ride my new bike?" she asked. "I spent all summer practising my 180 endo."

Remi waved her off. "We're in the third period of game seven of the Stanley Cup Finals. Marty promised to play out the series."

Trina pouted. She was used to getting her way.

So was my best friend. "Set up the net, Chan."

Torn between my promise to Remi and the chance to avoid his slap shots, I wasn't sure what to do. He must have sensed my hesitation because he yanked off his hockey gloves and tossed them to me.

"Here, these'll protect your hands," he said. "And use the oven mitt for your . . . you know."

I blushed, grinning sheepishly at Trina.

"Why are you guys playing *here*?" she asked. "Don't you know you're on crazy street?"

Remi squinted at the street sign. "No, we're on Riopel Road."

"*Hel-lo.* I'm not talking about addresses. I'm talking about that house." Trina pointed past her bike at the two-story red brick house surrounded by a lush green hedge. The sheer curtains in the top window flapped gently in the breeze. "That's the Asylum House."

Remi tilted his head to the side. "Asylum? What's that mean?"

"It's a place for crazy people," I explained. I remembered many of Batman's enemies ended up in an asylum.

Trina pulled us away from the curb. "Shhh! They'll hear you."

"Who?" I asked.

"The maniacs," Trina whispered.

"Go on," I said.

She led us across the street. "In 1983, a family moved into the house. The dad worked in Edmonton while the mom stayed at home with their twins, a boy and a girl. As soon as the dad left for work, weird things started to happen. Appliances broke down. The dishwasher made a horrible squealing noise; the washing machine sounded like a drum solo. The noise was so bad that the mom made her kids play outside while she called a handyman to fix the problem, but he couldn't fix the appliances. Ever."

"My dad's an electrician," Remi said. "I bet he could have fixed them."

She ignored him. "The parents fought about the weird things happening in the house. The mom wanted new machines and the dad blamed her for hiring a terrible handyman. The twins stayed in the playground while the parents argued. Then one night, the dad came home early. There was a lot of screaming and when the twins came home there was no mom. No dad. But the washing machine was making a horrible banging noise, so they went downstairs to check it. When they lifted the lid, what the kids saw was so gruesome that their hair turned white and they both went insane. People say the sister stayed locked in the attic, while her brother lived

13

on the main floor and picked his nose for a snot collection. People say that if you get too close to the house, the twins will drag you in and feed you to the washing machine."

The house looked much different now. The hedge's tiny brown claws reached out for me. The air went still and the curtains stopped moving. A strange metallic groan came from somewhere deep inside the house. We said nothing until the sound died. I backed away from the hedge.

"So do you guys still want to play hockey by the Asylum House, or do you want to go to the park and watch me ride my brand new mountain bike?"

"Show me that endo," I said, walking toward her.

"No way," Remi grabbed me by the back of my shirt. "She made up the story to scare you."

Trina's lips melted into a handlebar grimace. "Did not," she muttered.

"Remi, I'm tired," I whined. "And I don't want to get hurt."

"Don't quit on me, Chan. Coach says quitting is what cowards do. Coach says facing your fear builds character. Don't you want to build your character?"

"No. I want a cup."

Remi crossed his arms over his Toronto Maple Leafs jersey. "Grab the goalposts. Let's play."

I didn't want to let him down, but I also didn't want to be a human target any longer.

"Maybe Trina wants to play."

Her smile widened like the Cheshire Cat's. "Against Remi? I'd love to."

"She might get hurt," he muttered.

"Practise your wrist shot instead of the slap shot," I suggested.

"Coach says go all out or go home."

Trina grabbed the fly swatter from me. "You can go all out. I don't mind."

I handed her the hockey gloves. "You'll need these. He shoots pretty hard."

She sneered as she donned the gloves. "We'll see."

I set up the net several houses away from the Asylum House, placing the cans very far apart. I didn't want Trina to be hurt by Remi's slap shots.

"Are you cheating?" she accused. "Push the cans closer together."

"No, it's not what you think. I was moving them so —"

"Chan, I don't need your help," Remi said.

I nodded and moved the cans closer together.

"You ready, Brewster?"

She slapped one of the gloves against her leg and bent low, like a second baseman about to field a grounder. Remi wound up and fired. The crack of his stick hitting the puck rang out like he'd hit a home run. The puck whizzed toward the net. She snatched the black biscuit out of the air.

"I thought your coach said to go all out or go home," she said, tossing me the puck to take back to Remi.

I whispered, "Thanks for taking it easy on Trina."

He growled, dropped the puck on the pavement and fired a blistering slap shot. She whipped her glove beside her hip and caught the puck. She blew on her glove like she was blowing out a birthday candle.

He fired shot after shot, but Trina stopped them all. Every time she made a save she did a little goalie dance to taunt Remi. Sometimes, she raised her arms. Sometimes she stuck her butt out at Remi. Most times, she laughed.

He banged his stick on the pavement. "Okay, Brewster, you asked for it."

Instead of winding up, he charged the net. He deked left, then right, then left again. Trina crouched low and slammed her feet together, watching the Remi rocket hurtling toward her. She barely budged from the centre of the net. About ten feet away, he skidded to a halt and wound up.

"That's too close!" I yelled.

Too late, he brought his stick forward. Trina ducked. But the puck sat on the ground beside his feet. He had faked her out. He cracked a smug grin and tapped the puck past her and the pop can goalposts.

"He shoots! He scores!" Remi yelled as he lunged forward and speared the air in victory.

Trina threw the gloves on the ground and grabbed the stick.

"My turn," she said as she stick-handled the puck down the street and turned around. "Or are you chicken?"

He picked up the gloves from the pavement. "Coach says when you talk trash, you shoot garbage."

I wondered if his coach taught hockey or just came up with weird sayings.

"Ready?" she asked.

Remi yawned and waved her forward. She swung the stick back and took the shot. The taped blade jammed into the cement like a pelican diving for fish. The puck catapulted into the air, over the net and bounced down the street.

"She shoots! She scores!" yelled Trina.

"No way. Too high." He waved off the goal like a referee.

"Goalposts stretch to infinity," Trina claimed.

"Since when?"

"Since always," she said. "Isn't that right, Marty?"

My friends walked toward me.

"Marty, tell her it wasn't a goal," Remi ordered.

Trina smiled sweetly as she grabbed my arm. Goosebumps popped up all over my flesh. She whispered in my ear, "If you make the right call, I'll let you ride my bike."

"I heard that. You can't bribe the referee," Remi squawked.

I told the truth. "We play with regulation nets. No infinity posts. No goal."

She dug her fingers into my arm like a cat stapling its claws into a couch. Gone was her sweet grin.

"Think about your call."

I pulled away from her death grip. "The call stands. No goal."

Remi whooped and threw his arms up in victory. Trina booted one of the pop can goalposts as hard as she could. It clattered down the street. She stomped after it.

"Sore loser," he said. "She reminds me of Kyle's dad."

"You had more than one shot on goal. Shouldn't she have a few more tries?" I asked.

He shook his head. "No way. Game over."

"That's not fair," I said.

"Coach says life's not supposed to be fair."

"Did he really say that?"

He didn't answer.

"Remi, you owe Trina a fair chance," I said. "Or else people will say you're scared of losing to a girl."

He sighed. "Just because you're right doesn't mean you're getting out of playing net for the game seven finals. Hey, Trina, you get one more shot."

I nudged him in the ribs.

"A few more shots," he corrected himself.

If she heard us, she didn't look like she cared. She paced around the street, searching for something. Remi and I jogged after her.

"What's wrong?" I asked.

"Someone," Trina said, "stole my bike."

TWO

Trina ran along the sidewalk. Her head swung back and forth like she was watching a bouncing Superball. I followed her while Remi searched the other side of the street for the missing mountain bike.

I felt bad for her. I once lost my dad's car keys, while I was playing pirate. I knew Dad would make me walk the plank if he found out I was messing with his keys, and Mom'd send me to Davy Jones' locker if she noticed the key scratches on the side of her China cabinet. My stomach burned and my legs felt like electric eels as I combed the house for the keys and a brown pencil crayon to colour in the scratches.

Eventually, I found the keys buried under a stack of newspapers. If I'd taken my time, I probably would have remembered that I'd buried the treasure under the papers as part of the pirate adventure, but I was panicking, just like Trina was doing now.

"Slow down," I said. "You might miss a clue."

"My dad is going to be so mad at me," she said.

"Don't worry. We'll find your bike."

"He told me to look after it," she said, paying no attention to me. "He told me to lock it up. He told me he paid a lot of money for it and he wasn't going to buy me a new bike if I lost this one. He's going to ground me for a month."

"No, he won't." If her dad was anything like my dad, he'd ground her forever.

Her cheeks turned bright red. She chewed on her fingernails. She fidgeted from one foot to another like she had to pee. Then she grabbed my shirt.

"You have to help me find it!" she yelled.

"It's okay, Trina. We're going to find your bike."

"Why did you make me play hockey? If you didn't make me play, I'd still have my bike. This is your fault."

I tried to calm her down. "Let's think this through. If someone stole your bike, they had to have a good reason, right?"

Trina stopped. "I guess."

I waved Remi over.

"Do you know anyone who doesn't like you?" I asked her.

She gasped. "How dare you say that? Everyone likes me."

"How about the Graffiti Ghouls?" I asked.

The teenagers we'd caught spray-painting buildings last year might have held a grudge against Trina for turning them in to the police.

Remi shook his head. "My sister said those guys went to work in Halifax. No one's heard from them since July."

"Any other enemies?"

She shook her head.

"Maybe someone just wanted her bike," Remi suggested.

"Good point. It is a brand new bike," I said. "Trina, does anyone know you have a new bike?"

"I stopped at Eric Johnson's house before I came here. He wanted to ride my bike and he got upset when I wouldn't let him."

"Looks like we have a suspect," Remi said. "Let's find Eric."

My stomach fluttered and my heart pounded hard as we ran to Eric's house. My summer vacation was coming to an end, but a new mystery was beginning, and it promised to be more interesting than anything that might happen at school. Or so I thought.

According to my favourite cop shows, the way to squeeze a confession out of a crook was to make him think you already knew the truth. If the tactic worked on TV, it had to work in real life.

Eric crouched on his front lawn looking at the grass. He held something shiny in his hand.

"We're on to you, Eric," I barked, trying out the interrogation technique.

He spun around and hid his hands behind his back. "I wasn't doing anything."

Trina started to speak, but I shook my head. Remi picked up my signal and whispered in Trina's ear. She pursed her lips shut. I strolled toward Eric, taking my time and humming what I thought would sound like a cool theme song if I starred in a TV detective series.

"Why are you humming *Row, Row, Row Your Boat?*" Eric asked, peering at me through his long blond bangs.

Ignoring his comment, I flashed him the same interrogation stare my mom used on me whenever she thought I'd done something wrong. Once I accidentally broke her favourite vase, and she broke the confession out of me with an intense squint. I hoped I'd inherited her power of squint-errogation.

"Do you need to go to the bathroom?" he asked.

"I ask the questions. Not you," I barked.

Eric took a step forward. "Tough talk from a creep."

Normally a threat from him was enough to shut me up, but I felt safe with Remi and Trina backing me up. As long as they stood behind me, I felt like I was in total control. Squint-ensity level to eleven.

"You're already in trouble, Eric. Don't make it any worse. We know what you did."

He stepped back. "What do you know?"

"We saw you do it. You might as well admit it." I said. "Or we'll have to tell everyone about your nasty habit."

"There's no law against it."

Trina growled. "Yes there is. Tell me where you put it, or else I go to the police."

I cocked my head to the side, signalling to Remi. He nodded and tried to walk to the other side of Eric, while I flanked my prime suspect. I wanted to get a look at the thing behind his back, but he stepped away from both of us. I fixed my gaze on his face. He wouldn't look me in the eye, a sure sign of guilt. Sooner or later, he'd crack under the pressure.

"Trina's right," I said. "She wanted to go to the police right away, but I thought we should give you a shot at coming clean first."

"I'm not telling you anything."

"This could go very badly for you."

"Keep it up, Slanty Eyes. Might go worse for you," he growled.

I hated the name he called me, because it reminded me that I looked different than the rest of the kids in town, but after hearing the name so much, I learned the best thing to do was ignore it. Showing people that the name bothered me was like teasing a dog with a bone. Once the mutt saw the bone, he wouldn't stop until he had it. Eric was one dog I didn't want to tease.

Instead, I sighed and shook my head. "I guess we'll have to tell your mom."

He bit his lower lip. "You wouldn't."

Remi nodded. "You better believe we will."

Eric glanced back at his house, nervous.

"Are you going to come clean?" I asked.

Suddenly, he brought his right arm around as if he were going to rabbit punch me. I ducked, and waited for contact, but Eric wasn't throwing a punch. He was throwing something away.

"No evidence. No crime!" he yelled.

He dashed toward the back of the house as the thing he threw fell on the road. Trina bolted after him. Remi wasn't sure if he should follow them or stay with me.

"Get the evidence," I said.

"What about Trina?" Remi asked.

"Do you want to get in her way?"

He shook his head. Then he joined me as I ran to the street. Halfway across the road we found a magnifying glass. The lens was cracked and the handle was still damp from Eric's clammy hand.

"What's a magnifying glass have to do with a stolen bike?" Remi asked.

"I have no idea."

"Maybe he's on a crime spree," he guessed.

Something wasn't making sense. "Remi, if you had a choice between playing with a magnifying glass or riding a bike, what would you do?"

"The bike. No doubt."

"Me too. So why wasn't Eric doing that?"

He scratched his head. "I don't know. There had to be something more interesting on the lawn."

"When in doubt, ask the lawn," I said.

"Lawns don't talk."

I shook my head. "I meant there may be a clue."

"Oh," Remi said. "Why didn't you just say so?"

"I was trying to be dramatic."

"You're watching way too many TV shows."

We headed back to the house. I spotted a mound of dirt on the lawn where we first saw Eric. I held the cracked magnifying glass to the hill. A swarm of ants crawled across the mound, avoiding a few blades of grass that looked singed.

"I think he was trying to fry the ants," I said.

"That's terrible," Remi said. "What did ants ever do to him?"

Trina stomped around the corner of the house.

"He locked himself in the house," she said. "But he's got to come out sooner or later. What did he throw away?"

I held up the magnifying glass. "He was —"

Remi cut me off. "Burning ants. It's a sure sign that he's a criminal."

"The monster," Trina said. "What do you think he's going to do to my bike?"

"I heard that thieves chop up bikes and sell the parts."

"Wait a minute," I said. "We can't be sure Eric took your bike. I mean why would he take it and then not ride it?"

"Duh! He's hidden the bike," she said. "That way no one will suspect him of stealing it. Once no one's watching, he'll start riding the bike."

Remi nodded. "Or chop it up and make enough money to buy a different bike. That's what a smart thief would do."

"Have you met Eric Johnson?" I asked. "Smart and him go together like chocolate ice cream over steamed cauliflower."

She shook her head. "I bet he's playing dumb to throw us off the scent."

"Look at the burnt blades of grass. You'd have to hold the glass here for a long time," I said. "He wouldn't have time to steal your bike *and* burn the grass."

"He might have had an accomplice." Like a giant squid, she'd wrapped her tentacles around the idea of Eric being the criminal and she was dragging Remi down with her to the murky depths of her accusations.

"I think she's got a point," he offered. "Doesn't he have an older brother?"

"Yes, but you're jumping to conclusions," I said. "Why don't we go back to the scene of the crime and see if we missed anything? Eric isn't going to come out as long as we're standing here."

"If we leave he'll start chopping up the bike," Trina argued.

"Not if he thinks we're still watching him." I motioned Remi and Trina to follow me toward the front of the house. The drapes in the window were closed, but they moved slightly when we walked near the house. Eric was probably hiding behind the drapes.

"Trina, you watch the house from the alley," I yelled. "Remi and I will hide in the bushes and watch the front."

I grabbed Remi's hockey stick and waved it in front of the window for Eric to see. "We'll wave the stick if we see anything, Trina," I said, hoping Eric could hear us through the window.

"Okay," she finally said. "I'll be in the alley. You two hide in the bushes."

We walked away from the house to the bushes. I shoved the stick through the branches so the blade jutted out far enough for Eric to see it. As long as the hockey stick was there, he'd think we were watching him.

"Does that work for you?" I asked Trina.

She reluctantly agreed, and we left the house.

Back to the scene of the crime. We paced back and forth in front of the high hedge that protected the Asylum House. I didn't like being so close to the maniac twins, but we had to find the bike. I searched for clues with the cracked magnifying glass.

"I think you dropped the bike here," I said.

Trina pointed a few feet over. "No. See the indent in the grass? It was there."

"Where were you before you saw Eric?" Remi asked.

She blinked, trying to remember. "I think it was my uncle's gas station. There were a couple of teenagers outside the shop."

"Let's retrace your steps," I said. "Maybe we'll find another clue."

Remi patted her on the shoulder. "Don't worry. We'll find your bike."

She touched his arm. "I knew I could count on you."

My stomach clenched like I'd been hit by one of Remi's slap shots. I don't know why seeing Trina touch Remi bothered me, but it did. I started to follow the pair, but a sound stopped me: the faint jingle of a bicycle bell. I turned around and looked at the hedge. Was I hearing things? I tried to look through the leaves of the hedge, but the foliage was too thick. The bell jingled again. Could it be? No. Maybe.

Ring, ring. Yes. I was sure of it. The maniacs had stolen the bike.

THREE

"You can't be serious," Remi said. "You think Trina's bike is in the Asylum House?"

"I heard her bicycle bell behind the hedge," I said.

Remi and Trina leaned against the leafy wall and listened. Only silence came from the other side. Trina pulled away and squinted through the foliage. Remi burrowed into the hedge to get a better look.

"Ouch!" He pulled his hand away and sucked on his finger. "Thorns!"

"Quiet," I said.

More silence.

Trina turned away from the green wall. "Stop wasting our time, Marty. There's nothing in the yard."

"I'm serious. Someone was ringing your bicycle bell."

Remi joked, "I think you need your hearing checked."

"Let's look in the yard," I said.

"You two can waste your time. I'm going to make Eric give me back my bike and then I'm going to make him sorry he was ever born."

"What are you going to do to him?" he asked.

"You ever see that show, *Robot Rampage*?"

"The one where robots smash each other into a thousand tiny little pieces?" I asked.

She cracked an evil grin and walked away.

"Remind me never to get on her bad side."

"She'll cool off. We have to see what's in the yard."

"Sounds like a stake out." Remi grinned. "We'll need some gear."

"I know just the place to find it," I said.

My parents' grocery store doubled as our home. The good news: I had twenty-four hour access to any chocolate bar in the milk chocolate galaxy. The bad news: my dad only let me eat the meteorite-hard Mojos which hadn't sold in over two years. The worst news: I had a universe of chores. I had to sweep the floors not only in our living quarters but also in the entire store. Taking out the garbage took almost an hour, because I had to break down cardboard boxes for the recycle bin. By the end of my daily chores, I was covered in dust and paper cuts.

But today I was glad to live in a grocery store, because I could borrow equipment for the stake-out. I needed a note pad, a couple of pens and a pair of binoculars. I had the pad and pens in my room, but the binoculars were on a dusty shelf in the store. Dad had bought the binoculars hoping that Mr. Chalifoux, the president of the Bouvier Birdwatchers' Club, would pick them up, but Mr. Chalifoux already had a pair, as did everyone else in the Bouvier Birdwatchers' Club. The binoculars sat on the shelf collecting dust. Today they'd finally get some good use.

"What do we do if your parents catch us?" Remi asked, glancing around the store nervously.

My parents never liked Remi, and he didn't want to make things worse, especially after he'd tasted one of Mom's delicious homemade egg rolls.

"Tell them we're getting a jump on our school work," I said as I pulled the binoculars out of their hard leather case.

"They sure like it when you study."

I moaned, "If Dad had his way, he'd chain me to a table so I could do school work all day. The only time he'd let me out is to do chores and go to the bathroom. If they made diapers my size, I think he'd only let me out to do chores."

"What do we say about the binoculars?"

"They're for a science project," I said.

"You're getting good at lying," Remi said. "Almost too good. I think you've been hanging around Monique too much."

His older sister ruled the kingdom of lies. This queen of fibs made up fake stories and excuses to explain why she missed curfew, why she didn't finish her homework or why Remi had to be her slave.

"Do you know what we need for a real stake out?" Remi asked.

I shrugged.

"Doughnuts. I see the cops in television shows eating powdered doughnuts all the time. What do you think, Marty?"

"How does eating doughnuts help catch criminals?"

He shrugged. "Dunno. But they're so swweeeeet."

"Sorry, Remi. If you want doughnuts, you have to buy them."

"Can I get a family discount?" he asked. "We're practically brothers."

"You can ask my dad."

He shook his head. "Never mind. Don't take this the wrong way, but he scares me sometimes."

"Sometimes? My dad scares me all the time."

Lately, Dad wanted me to work in the store instead of hanging out with Remi. Now that I was older he wanted me to do more chores so he wouldn't have to hire a stock boy. Unlike Remi's sister, my dad didn't need to tell any lies to make me his slave.

"Keep an eye out for my parents," I said.

I reached for the binoculars.

"*Die Gaw*," he mumbled.

I pulled my hand back. *Die Gaw* was code that meant someone was watching us. *Die Gaw* was Chinese for "big brother." Over the summer we'd started using Chinese words for code phrases to keep the French and English kids from guessing what we were saying. But I never counted on my parents hearing the code phrase.

Dad walked up, rolling up the sleeves of his white dress shirt. He swept the few strands of his hair over his balding top as he looked at Remi like he was eyeing a shoplifter.

"Why did your friend call you big brother?" Dad asked.

"I'm teaching him some Chinese," I said.

"Did I say it right, Mr. Chan?" Remi asked.

"You're not related," he barked.

So much for the family discount.

"Homework," we answered at the same time.

"School hasn't started yet."

"Uh . . . I heard about what I need to do from the kids who were in grade five last year," I said.

Remi backed me up. "We wanted to get a head start on our school work, Mr. Chan."

"S'waw ji," Dad muttered.

"Pardon?"

I wasn't about to tell Remi what my dad had called him.

"Marty, tell your friend to go home. It's time to work. I need you to stock the shelves."

"Can I do it later?" I asked.

Dad glared at me, his nostrils flaring.

Remi inched away. "I'll see you later."

"Can he help?" I asked.

Dad shook his head. "This is your job. If your friend works, I'll have to pay him."

"How come you don't have to pay Marty?" Remi asked.

Dad shot him a dirty look. A tiny vein on his forehead started to bulge out, the sign that my dad was getting really upset. Only I knew this sign, because of all the times Dad got mad at me.

My dad gritted his teeth. "Marty gets paid with the clothes on his back and the food on his table."

I wanted to point out that Remi got clothes and food from his parents too and he didn't have to do as many chores, but I knew better than to question Dad, especially not when his vein was popping out.

"I'll see you tomorrow," I told Remi.

He nodded and ran out of the store. I went to the stockroom to pick up boxes, wishing my dad could ease up on the chores, but there was no arguing with him. I suspected he thought that if we looked busy in the store, the customers would feel sorry for us and come buy some groceries. I worked hard, hoping to get the next day's chores done in one night.

The next morning I snuck out of the store with my detective gear before Dad found more work for me to do. I had no intention of spending the rest of my summer cooped up in my dad's store collecting paper cuts.

Stakeout Report
Detectives: Remi Boudreau and Marty Chan
Subject: The Asylum House

3:00 pm   Detectives met across the street from the Asylum House. Remi kept repeating "Asylum" and laughing.

3:15 pm   Observed hedge. No movement. No sound of bicycle.

3:22 pm   Observed hedge. No one moving. No sound. Remi said he was bored.

3:31 pm   Watching the hedge, but nothing is moving. Remi starts a flinch war. Marty loses bad. Remi punches him in the shoulder and Marty cries like a baby. Remi is the king of flinch wars. Marty pees his pants. Marty is the king of peeing his pants. All hail the king of peed pants.

3:36 pm   Remi is no longer allowed to touch the official detective scribbler when I go on a bathroom break.

3:41 pm   Observed hedge. No movement. No sound.

3:56 pm   Car stops in front of hedge. Boy climbed out of the passenger side. He dropped something on the ground and got back into the car.

3:57 pm Car drove away. A flyer for household appliances was left on the sidewalk beside the hedge. Remi believed the maniac twins might come out to get the flyer.

4:11 pm Observed hedge. Remi thought he heard something. Nothing.

4:14 pm Observed hedge. I heard something. Remi said I was making fun of him.

4:17 pm Observed hedge. We both heard Trina's bicycle bell.

4:23 pm We plan to move in. If we don't come back, please get this report to Trina Brewster. She will know what to do.

Remi led the way toward the hedge. He crouched low and scuttled across the pavement like a crab. I tucked the scribbler in the back of my pants and followed. Instead of following, I edged along the hedge to the side of the house until I reached the alley that ran beside the house. Then I crept down the alley to a wooden gate. I lowered myself on my hands and knees and peeked under the gate. Pebbles dug into my palms and the ground smelled a little like rotten cabbage, most likely from the garbage cans beside the gate.

A brick walkway on the other side of the gate led to the house. Tall grass threatened to crawl over the red brick path. I thought I saw the hint of a bicycle wheel in the distance, but I couldn't be sure what I saw, because on the other side of the fence, someone was walking toward the gate.

I pushed up from the ground, but the sleeve of my T-shirt snagged on the bottom of the fence. I tried to pull away, but the T-shirt was stuck. The feet drew closer.

A maniac twin was about to find me.

FOUR

The black shoes clopped across the brick path, moving closer to the gate. I yanked at the T-shirt sleeve, trying to free myself, but the cloth had turned as slippery as a non-stick frying pan and my French fry fingers couldn't grab hold. The maniac twin was right at the gate.

I rolled away, tearing my sleeve. Just as the cedar gate swung open I curled into a ball with my back to the hedge. A man stepped into the alleyway with a huge green garbage bag. His back to me, he tossed the bag into the aluminium garbage can. The first thing that grabbed my attention was his crazy white hair. I held my breath, expecting him to turn around. As I waited, time became a caterpillar inching along a highway to a rest stop called Trouble. I closed my eyes and waited for the ride to end.

"What are you doing there?" the man shouted.

The sound of his voice skidded across my ears like tires screeching across a highway. I opened my eyes.

"You! What are you doing with those binoculars?" The maniac still had his back to me. All I could see was his bushy white hair. Down the alley, Remi was looking at the maniac through the binoculars.

"Are you spying on me?" the man asked.

Remi lowered the binoculars. "No. I was just playing around."

"Come here," the man ordered. "Did Davis send you?"

Remi backed up.

"I want to talk to you."

"Maybe another time."

"What did Davis pay you to do this?" The maniac walked away from me.

I could breathe again. Remi, on the other hand, was in big trouble. I waved to my pal to run. He started to jog away.

"Don't you even think about running," the man yelled.

Remi paused, looked back at me, and then bolted. The maniac started to chase after him, leaving me free to make my escape. As I stood up, I noticed the maniac's yard was filled with junk. There was more metal than grass behind the hedge. I wanted to take a closer look, but the sound of footsteps scared me. I hid behind the open gate and peeked between the slats.

The white-haired man had stopped chasing Remi. Now he walked back toward me, scratching his salt and pepper beard. I needed to find a better hiding spot. I slid behind the garbage can and crouched down, balancing on the balls of my feet. I wobbled as he got closer and grabbed the can to steady myself. It rocked back an inch. I took a deep breath and got a snoot full of mouldy cheese and rotting cabbage. I held my breath wishing I hadn't picked such a stinky hiding place.

A hand reached around the gate. A few inches away, the white-haired maniac was about to go into his yard. *Close the gate*, I thought. *Just close the gate.* I shifted on the ground to maintain my balance, but as I did my arm bumped against the can. *Clang.*

The white-haired man held the gate open and looked right at me. For the first time I saw his eyes. They were huge and round, like fish eyes.

"Spy!" he yelled.

I jumped up, knocked the can over and ran up the alley. Behind me, a loud metal crash and a scream filled the air. I wondered if the maniac had unleashed the washing machine monster. I sprinted for freedom. As I ran I imagined the monster behind me, reaching out to nab my torn shirt and put me through the rinse-and-munch cycle. This thought gave me the energy to sprint all out.

I ran to the end of the block, cut through three yards, hopped over four fences, zipped past two barking dogs and crossed the street. Finally I came to a stop near a maple tree at the end of a quiet road. I leaned against the tree trunk to catch my breath. No sign of the maniac twin. I was safe.

A hand reached around the tree and grabbed my sweaty T-shirt. Another hand clamped around my mouth to keep me from screaming. Washing machine, here I come.

"Shhhh," Remi hissed. "It's me."

Once I relaxed, my friend released me.

"You okay?"

I nodded. "Did you see the guy's eyes? They were so buggy. I've never seen anything like them. Have you?"

He shook his head. "I don't want to see them ever again."

"If you hadn't distracted him, I'd be dirty laundry," I said.

"You were lucky I spotted you going around the corner."

"Thanks. I owe you one," I said. Actually, I owed him 53 times for the times he saved me from sticky situations. The good thing was he never kept count and he never asked for anything in return.

"Did you see Trina's bike in the yard?"

I shook my head. "I saw some big gears and wheels and I think I saw a refrigerator, but no bike."

"What would he want with all that stuff?"

"Maybe the monster needs a bigger washing machine."

Remi nodded and looked up the street.

"We'd better tell Trina," I said.

"She won't believe us," he said. "Not until we get her proof."

"We have to get into that yard," I said.

He bit his lower lip. I could tell he was trying to figure out if I was as crazy as the white-haired maniac.

"What's your plan?" he asked.

"We're going to sneak in."

The plan was simple: wait for the maniac to leave. However, he wasn't going anywhere. We could hear him behind the hedge, hammering and using a power saw. The whine of the blade loosened my back teeth and I had to cover my ears until the noise stopped. By then it was time for dinner. We'd have to try again tomorrow.

The next day was a repeat of the first day: all noise and no action. The waiting reminded me of how I felt when I waited for my tooth to fall out. Part of me wanted the tooth to come out, but another part wanted the tooth to stay in. When I wiggled the tooth, I could speed up the process, but there was no way I could wiggle Mr. White Hair.

At the end of the stake out, Remi whined, "He's not coming out, and I'm bored. Let's play street hockey while we're waiting."

Maybe there *was* a way to wiggle Mr. White Hair. "Do you have a puck?"

"Yup. We can use some branches for sticks."

"Hand me the puck," I said.

He dug into his pocket and pulled out the puck. I grabbed it and walked to the hedge around the Asylum House.

"Are you going to ask him to play hockey with us?"

I explained my plan. Remi would hide next to the gate while I launched a puck over the hedge. I would throw the puck into the middle of the yard. Mr.

White Hair would notice it and charge out looking for the puck's owner. I would taunt the maniac until he chased me and Remi would look for the bike in the maniac's yard. We'd hope that the other maniac twin never came out of the attic.

I gave my pal the signal. Then I wound up and hurled the puck high into the air with every ounce of my strength. The black biscuit landed on the ground barely a foot in front of me. I wiped my hands on my pants, picked up the puck, charged at the hedge and tossed the puck again. This time it landed behind me.

Remi jogged over. "Let me do it," he suggested.

"I can throw the puck," I said. "My hands were slippery, that's all."

"I'd like to get in the yard before the sun goes down." He grinned.

"Fine, fine. Go ahead."

I ran to the hiding place beside the gate and signalled Remi to throw the puck. He launched it high over the hedge and sprinted away. Crack! Did he break a window? The yard went silent. I crouched, waiting for Mr. White Hair to come out so I could sneak into the yard. A minute passed. Two minutes. Three minutes. I straightened up as Remi peeked around the corner of the hedge. I shrugged. He waved me over.

"Do you have something else I can throw? Maybe the puck was too little."

"There's no way he could have missed it, Remi. It sounded like you broke his window."

A shrill whine came from behind the hedge. We scrambled away as a loud buzz followed. The buzz and whine faded away. Then something black flew over the hedge and plopped on the sidewalk. It was *half* the puck. Behind the hedge the sounds of hammering and grinding started up again.

Remi grabbed the half puck and examined the cut. "Gee, I wonder if he does that to everything that ends up in his yard."

I looked at the mangled biscuit and gulped.

"Do you think Trina's bike is worth this?" Remi asked.

I wasn't going to give up. I wanted to see Trina's face light up when I returned her stolen bike. I wanted to see her flash that special smile for me and no one else. But I didn't want Remi to know how I felt. He'd make fun of me if he knew the truth.

So I stalled for time. "Well, we can't do anything until next weekend anyway. School starts tomorrow."

He groaned. "Did you have to remind me about school?"

We agreed to show Trina our detective report and made plans to meet in the schoolyard. That night I couldn't sleep. I tossed and turned in my bed like one of the over-cooked sausages Mom made for breakfast. When my alarm clock went off, I knew I was done with sleep. While I wasn't looking forward to starting grade five, I was excited to have a chance to sit near Trina. I only wished I'd found her bike before school started.

That morning I scanned the schoolyard for Remi. I expected to find him on the French side of the schoolyard. Our school was split into French and English classes, which gave all the students an excuse to wage schoolyard battles. The war meant that no French kid could hang out with an English kid. There'd be purple nurples for anyone who broke the code. To make sure no one made any mistakes, the kids used to split the schoolyard down the middle: half for the French, half for the English.

That was last year. This year, the warring sides had declared a truce. While the younger students still divided themselves into French and English groups, all the grade five and six students were hanging out together. The older students seemed less interested in who was French and who was English and more interested in who had the best hair and who had the cutest smile.

In the middle of one group, Remi was talking to Trina. What was he doing with her? We had agreed to talk to her together. I jogged over, but the bell rang before I could reach them. At least Trina and I would have some alone time in class. Remi had to go to the French side for his classes.

Our new classroom was nothing like the grade four room. Instead of pictures of kittens and puppies, there were photos of galaxies. No fancy handwriting anywhere. Everything was printed and taped to the whiteboard. Science models, like a homemade light box and a model of the solar system, sat on the back counter. The teacher's desk looked like the control room for a space shuttle mission.

I sat in the desk right behind Trina. She barely noticed me as she glared at the back of Eric Johnson's blond head. He played his handheld video game, ignoring her dagger glare.

"We're going to get your bike back, Trina," I promised.

She said nothing. She watched a couple of boys gather around Eric. Trina glared right through them. There was no talking to her while she was in this mood. Instead, I pulled out my lime-green scribbler. I flipped it open to the back. I doodled my secret thoughts on the inside back cover.

I used ultra-secret codes and doodles that captured how I was feeling. Across the top of the cover, a lot of my doodles were of Maple Leafs, which I had started to draw after Remi and I became friends and I learned that the Toronto Maple Leafs were his favourite hockey team. Today, I moved to the bottom of the cover and started to draw little hearts. Inside each heart, I wrote "M.C. plus T.B." I was pretty sure no one would ever be able to crack my code, because the print was so small only I could read it. I drew the hearts as far away from the Maple Leafs as possible.

Trina turned around finally. I shut my scribbler fast.

"Eric's so smug, but he's going to crack sooner or later," Trina said.

"Did Remi say anything to you?" I asked.

"When?"

"This morning. I thought I saw you talking to him."

"Yes. He said he was going to get my bike for me."

"Both of us are going to help," I said. "I have notes."

"Trust me, Marty. I'm looking at the thief," she said, not taking her eyes off Eric.

The classroom door swung open and a man entered the room.

"Budding lovers of science," he said. "I'm going to show you that geek is chic. My name is Mr. Eisenberg, your teacher and guide for the year. However, I understand the temptation to mispronounce it as Iceberg or Izzybug, so instead I give you permission to refer to me as Mr. E."

Mr. E wore a white lab coat over his suit, but the most shocking things about him were his spiky white hair and his bulging fish eyes. My mouth nearly dropped open. My new teacher was none other than Mr. White Hair — the maniac.

FIVE

I hid behind the lime-green scribbler, hoping my teacher wouldn't recognize me. I wished I could turn into one of the doodles in my scribbler. Instead, I tried to shrink in my desk.

"Now that you know my name, it's time I got to know yours," my teacher said, scanning his attendance sheet.

This guy seemed nothing like the puck mangler from the Asylum House. I started to wonder if he was the suspect. I wished Remi were here so he could tell me if this was the guy.

"Trina Brewster," Mr. E called.

"Present."

"Quick. How many planets in the solar system?"

"Nine," she said. "Everyone knows that."

"Are you sure?"

"Positive."

"I'll mark you down as a nine."

He picked up a magnetic card with a "9" on the front and pinned the card to the board. Then he wrote Trina's name under the card.

"Elizabeth Carroll," he continued.

"It's Liz," said the red-haired girl in the row next to mine. She was Elizabeth in grade four, but she'd shortened her name over the summer along with her red hair.

Mr. E tapped the board. "Do you agree with Trina Brewster?"

Liz looked at Trina and slowly nodded.

"Really?" Mr. E wrote Liz's name on the board. "Is Marty Chan here?"

I kept the green scribbler in front of my face and raised my hand.

"Do you have a face or should I assume the scribbler speaks for you?" he asked.

I shook no with the scribbler. The other kids snickered, but I wasn't going to drop my scribbler mask.

"That's alright. Marie Curie was shy too, and she won two Nobel Prizes," Mr. E said. "For physics and chemistry. Can you imagine that?"

I nodded yes with the scribbler. The kids laughed.

"Let's move on."

I breathed a sigh of relief.

"Hannah Dalton," Mr. E said.

"Present." Hannah always wore pink blouses and with her spiky blond hair, she almost looked like a living Troll doll.

"Name the planets for me, Hannah."

"Um. There's Earth. And Mars. Venus. Jupiter. Saturn. Mercury. Neptune. And, uh . . . uh . . . " Hannah stumbled, trying to remember the other planet names.

"Uranus!" Eric shouted.

Everyone laughed.

"What's your name, son?"

"Eric Johnson."

"Tell me something. What do you think of science, Eric?"

"It's okay."

"I don't believe you," Mr. E said. "What do you really think of science? Come on, the truth."

"Well, it's kind of boring."

"Oh?" Mr. E walked toward Eric and picked up the video game from his desk. "Do you find your PSP boring?"

"No, it's awesome," Eric said.

"Did you know that the people who made your game were scientists?"

"Really?"

Mr. E nodded. "And they were into math and computers. In fact, they needed those skills to make the game you think is awesome. If you guys prove to me that you're good, I might even let you build some electric games yourselves. So now what do you think of science?"

Eric paused for a second, and then answered, "I still think it's boring. I'd rather play a game than make it."

"It looks like I have my work cut out for me. Eric, by the end of this year, I'm going to make you a science lover."

Beside Eric, a girl with purple streaks in her black hair muttered, "Good luck."

Mr. E shot her a dirty look and shook his head. "Scientists have a sense of humour," he said to Eric. "After all, it was scientists who named the planets. What was the name of that planet again?"

"Uranus!"

Mr. E laughed along with the rest of the class. Only the black-haired girl didn't laugh. She adjusted the sleeves of her black leather jacket.

"Ida, we seem to be one short of Trina's list of nine. Can you name the last planet on her list?"

As Ida pulled up her sleeve, she showed off a cotton wristband that had a doodle on it of a skull and crossbones. I was pretty sure she was new at school. I would have remembered someone with that much attitude. She rolled her eyes.

"That's inappropriate dress code. Take off the wristband."

She didn't budge.

"Now."

She lowered her hand below her desk and pulled off the wristband, glaring at our teacher.

Mr. E turned to the rest of the class. "So, what is the ninth planet?"

Trina shot a hand up. "Pluto!"

"He's a cartoon dog," Mr. E said.

"It's a planet too," Trina said.

"He could also be the Greek god of the underworld," he said, smiling.

"It's the ninth planet."

"Not any more. A bunch of astronomers got together in Prague and voted to kick Pluto out of the solar system club. They said if Pluto was a planet, then they'd have to accept another celestial body just past Pluto – UB313. And they said if that happened, then any Tom, Dick and Halley's Comet could join the club."

Everyone gaped at Mr. E with disbelief.

He continued, "You know when your family has Thanksgiving dinner and sometimes there's not enough room at the dining table, so the kids have to eat at a different table?"

A few of the kids nodded. I never had that problem because my parents never invited anyone over for Thanksgiving dinner. We all ate at the same table, but the way my dad chewed with his mouth open and the way my mom slurped chow mein noodles, I wouldn't have minded sitting at another table.

"Pluto was moved to the kids' table. The astronomers called Pluto a dwarf planet, because they said it was too small to be at the big table. Some astronomers put up a huge fight to keep Pluto at the grown-up table, but they lost. So now all our textbooks have to be changed. Isn't that cool? Science is always changing how we look at things. Never trust your first impression. You can be a rebel in science. That's why geek is chic."

Everyone smiled. Some nodded. But I wondered if this was the crazy maniac who had stolen Trina's bike. Our teacher continued to take attendance and then spent the rest of the time talking about how he was going to make science come to life. I didn't really listen. Instead, I kept staring at the clock, hoping recess would come soon so I could tell Remi everything.

When the recess bell finally rang, I put my hand over my face and stood up along with everyone else.

Mr. E shot his hand up and said, "Whoa, whoa."

We all stopped in our tracks. I kept my hand over my face.

"You're not Pavlov's dogs, are you?"

Everyone looked at each other, confused.

"Pavlov trained his dogs to drool every time a bell rang. They had no control over it, and they couldn't think for themselves. In this class, I want free thinkers, which means you can't be slaves to the bell. When it rings, fight the instinct to get up and run. Because if you let the bell run your life, that means you're no better than dogs."

"I like dogs," Eric said.

"Then I'll get a kennel for you to sit in," Mr. E said. Everyone laughed.

"Now, go and enjoy recess. But next time, don't let the bell turn you into drooling dogs. You're better than that."

I blended in with the crowd and made my way out of the classroom.

At first, Remi scoffed at the idea that my grade five teacher was the crazy white-haired man who lived in the Asylum House.

"How come we didn't see Mr. White Hair at school before this year?" Remi asked. "And what kind of name is Mr. E? What do you think his real name is?"

"Eisen . . . Einstein . . . Eisner . . . something that started with 'E.' Remember how he thought we were working for someone named Davis?"

"Yeah, but what's Davis have to do with our school?"

I shrugged. "Maybe that's the first name of one of our teachers. You know how everyone is a mister or miss."

"Or Madame," Remi added. "Yeah. You think that one of our teachers' first names is Davis?"

I nodded. "And he's looking for him." I said, pointing across the schoolyard at my teacher.

Remi ducked behind me and peeked from under my armpit at the white-haired teacher who seemed to be having a serious talk with the new girl, Ida.

"That's him, isn't it?" I asked.

"Yup." Remi said.

"I don't think he recognized me," I said. "At the house, he must not have gotten a good look."

"Yeah, but he saw me."

"You'll never see him as long as you stick to your side of the school."

"Let's get out of sight in case you're wrong."

I walked to a grove of trees, while Remi clung to my back like a baby spider monkey.

When I was sure Mr. E couldn't see us, I stepped away from my friend. Remi laid flat on his belly. I joined him on the ground to spy on our suspect. Mr. E walked away from Ida and went into the school. She stuck her tongue out at him as he headed into the brick building.

"What are we going to do about Mr. E?" I asked. "He's going to figure out we were the ones who threw the puck in his yard."

Remi scrunched his forehead and thought. He forgot to breathe when he thought, which is why I never let him think for very long.

"Maybe we can tell him that our street hockey game got out of control," I said.

Remi let out his breath in one whoosh. "Good idea, Marty. Blame my slap shot. Everyone knows my shot can go wild."

"But try staying away from him first. I don't want to get in trouble with a teacher this early in the school year."

Remi nodded. "Okay, I'll be careful. Did you know what Trina said this morning?"

"Were you talking to her?" I asked, pretending I hadn't seen them together.

"She might be right about Eric," he said. "He's been acting suspicious."

"Did she say anything else? Anything about me?"

Remi scrunched his face at me. "Why? Do you like Trina?"

"No way," I said. "Why would you ask that? She's a girl. Ew."

"The way you act around her makes me think you don't mind she's a girl. That maybe you like-*like* her."

"Trust me, Remi. I do not like-*like* Trina Brewster."

"Are you sure you don't like-*like* her?"

"I swear I don't like-*like* her. I barely like her as a friend."

Remi rolled on his side. "That's good. Because I think *I* kind of like-*like* her."

His slapshot confession smacked me right in the chest and hurt a million times more than a real shot. I wished there was a jockstrap for my heart. I tried to change the subject. "We should get Trina to help us stake out Mr. E's house."

"Are you sure we heard Trina's bike bell behind the hedge? There were a lot of weird noises coming from the yard."

Could Remi be right? Maybe I misheard the sound.

"Why would a teacher steal a bike? That's like saying that a cop steals."

He was right. When Mr. E was the crazy man in the Asylum House, he could have been a suspect, but teachers didn't steal. They yelled. They gave too much homework. They handed out detentions. But they didn't steal.

"Take him off the suspect list," I said.

"Come on, Marty. I need your help to tail Eric. We have to get Trina's bike back for her, and that means following solid leads."

He made sense. Plus, whoever found Trina's bike would be her hero. The only problem was that *I* wanted to be that hero.

"So will you help me?"

I didn't know what to tell him. I hated that he like — liked Trina. I hated myself even more for not telling him that I like — liked her. Maybe if I'd told him when I had the chance, he would have never told me how he felt. Now it was too late.

"Sure," I promised. "I'll help."

"I knew I could count on my best friend," he said, slapping me on the back.

Secretly I wished Trina would find the bike herself.

SIX

According to Trina, criminals always went back to the scene of the crime. Our job was to follow Eric everywhere in the hope that he'd lead us to Trina's stolen bike. In old detective movies, Remi and I would have been the flatfoots, the guys who pounded the pavement after suspects until our feet were flat. Remi didn't mind the boring work as long as he got to hand in the reports to Trina. He didn't like writing the reports though, which left me with the paperwork.

Case File

Stake out of Suspect Number One

By Detective Chan, assisted by Detective Boudreau

Tuesday: Subject showed video game to group
             of grade five boys. Subject did not let

anyone play, but allowed them to watch him play.

Wednesday: Subject bragged about the games he was going to buy. Question: where was subject getting the money? Detective Boudreau would like the record to show that he thinks the money was coming from stolen bikes.

Thursday: Subject picked empty pop bottles from a garbage can after school. He then washed the gold Cadillac that belongs to his grandma, Mrs. Johnson, the oldest driver in the world. Detective Chan would like the record to show that the subject might be earning money by doing odd jobs.

Friday: Subject told by the mad science teacher to stop playing game in the hallway, because too many boys were crowded around Eric and no one could get past the group. Detectives Boudreau and Chan agree that my teacher's fish eyes are creepy looking.

Saturday: Subject mowed four lawns. He accidentally mowed down a flower garden and said several bad words. Subject's grandfather caught him.

Sunday: Subject stayed inside house. Detective Boudreau asked why Detective Chan was drawing hearts on the stake out report. Chan said he was bored.

Monday: Subject ran into Trina in the schoolyard. She demanded that he return her bike. Subject said he did not take it and told her a bad word. Detective Boudreau is leaving his hiding position.

I grabbed Remi before he could blow our cover. Even though Eric had sworn at Trina, we had to stick to our job, but Remi couldn't hide his feelings. He wanted to protect her. What he didn't understand was that she could take care of herself. She muttered something to Eric that made him turn white and walk away.

Once Eric was gone, we approached Trina.

"What do you have to report?" she demanded.

"Nothing new," Remi said.

"You've said that every day," she barked. "I want answers. I'm sick of hearing that there's nothing new."

Remi's gaze darted from side to side, searching for something, anything to say to cool her off. I jumped in to help.

"We don't know anything yet, because you're always on Eric about the bike," I said. "Maybe if you backed off a bit."

She glared at me. "How should I back off?"

"You could apologize," I suggested.

"You want me to apologize to Eric?!"

"Yes," I said, feeling the heat of her anger taking off.

"I want justice." The way Trina said *justice* made me think justice had something to do with Eric's nose and a crash landing.

"It's just that . . . "

Remi cut me off before I could finish. "Trina, as long as you're breathing down Eric's neck, he'll never let his guard down."

"That's what I was trying to say," I said.

She sighed. "Okay, I'll trust you, Remi."

"It was my idea," I said, but no one listened. I started to feel like I felt before I met Remi and Trina: alone and invisible.

"Thanks." He blushed. Why didn't he say it was my idea? He continued, "You gotta convince Eric he's off the hook. Ask him to help you find the bike."

"What if he says yes?" Trina asked.

"If he took the bike, the last thing he'll want to do is help," I started to explain.

"It's part of my trap." Remi cut me off.

"Pretty good trap," Trina said, smiling.

He blushed again and looked down at his feet. My face turned red too, but for another reason. He was stealing my thunder.

"You have to make Eric think you think someone else took your bike," I said.

"I know. I could make Eric think I have another suspect," she said.

Remi nodded. "Good idea, Trina."

"I just *said* that," I exclaimed.

"But who do I accuse?" she asked.

Remi pointed at me. "Say Marty's the thief. Will you help, Marty?"

The way he kept taking credit for my ideas was making it hard to keep my promise to help him, but a promise was a promise. "Sure."

"Thanks, Marty," she said. "Good idea, Remi."

He blushed. "It's really Marty who's gonna do all the hard work."

He cracked a smile at me. He hadn't forgotten me. Before we could put our plan into action, however, Eric waded into the middle of our group and stuck his nose in Trina's face. His eyes were red, like he'd been crying. His fists were clenched and he was panting.

"*Hel-lo*, you're breathing my air," she said.

"Give it back," he demanded.

"Give what back?" she asked.

Remi shoehorned his arm between the two and warned, "Get back."

"Get out of my way, French Toast!" he yelled.

"Easy, Eric. We didn't do anything to you. What do you want?" I asked.

"She stole my video game!"

Trina took a step at him. I nabbed her arm to hold her back. Remi and I were like referees trying to stop a hockey brawl. I could barely hold on to Trina as she charged ahead. My shoes skidded across the grass as she dragged me forward.

"Why do you think Trina took your game?" I asked.

Eric wiped his eyes and said, "Because she thinks I stole her stupid bike. She stole my game for revenge."

"How could she? You go everywhere with it," I said.

"Mr. E made me put it away in my locker this morning. When I went to get it at lunch, the game was gone."

"I don't want your stupid game," Trina barked. "I want my bike back."

"Thief!" he barked.

"I know Trina, and she'd never steal," Remi argued. "Isn't that right, Marty?"

I was just about to back him up, when another idea struck me.

"I don't know about never stealing," I said.

"What!?" Trina turned on me.

"I knew it!" Eric shouted.

"Remi, don't you remember that time?" I asked, then I muttered. "*Mung koi gu ghewk,*" as I swatted my right ear twice and coughed into my left armpit, hoping my friend would pick up on the code phrase for "pull his leg".

He nodded. "Oh you mean that time," he said, catching on to my code. "You mean the time Trina took your . . . your . . . "

"Backpack. She stole my backpack," I said.

"I never stole anything in my entire life," she said, her nostrils now big enough to fit the moon.

"Of course you did," I lied. "I checked the Harry Potter book out of the library right before you got to the counter. You were steaming mad because *you* wanted to read it first."

"Did you hit your head this morning? *Hel-lo*, I own all the Harry Potter books."

Remi backed me up. "Yeah. Trina was really upset and then the next day, your backpack was gone."

Eric glared at her. "Once a thief, always a thief."

"Trina said the only way she would give it back was if I let her have the book," I said.

"Lies!"

Remi urged her to go along with my scheme, winking twice at her from behind Eric's back.

"Trina, you had a pretty good plan to get the book from Marty," Remi said. "He handed the book over when you threatened to cut his backpack."

She smiled as she caught on, but looked down at the ground quickly so that Eric wouldn't notice. "Sooner or later, I always get what I want, even if I have to get nasty."

"I'd hate to think what you'd do to Eric's video game," I said.

"Hmm, if I did have the game, I'd probably put it under my dad's car just before he went to work so that he could run over it."

"No." Eric whined.

"I'll bet if you give her bike back, she'll give you your game back."

"If I have your game," Trina corrected me.

He fell on his knees and put his hands together. "Don't destroy the game. I'll do anything you want. Just name it. Please."

"Where's my bike, Eric?"

He hung his head. "I don't know."

"She'll bust your game," Remi said.

Eric looked up, his eyes filling with tears. "I swear, Trina. I didn't touch your bike."

She wasn't ready to back down. She pulled her backpack off her shoulder and threw it on the ground in front of him. Then she raised her foot over the pack.

"Your game's in there. Where's my bike?"

"I told you I don't know."

Trina stomped the backpack. Eric screamed and pushed Trina's foot away, while he grabbed the pack. He opened it and dumped the contents out. Scribblers fell out along with a pencil case and two textbooks. But there was no video game.

"I thought you said my PSP was in the backpack," Eric said.

She shook her head. "I never took your game."

I nodded. "The backpack thing was a lie."

"You jerks," Eric said, climbing to his feet.

"What about my bike?" she asked.

"I hope whoever took it throws it under your dad's car," Eric said as he ran away.

"You didn't fall for that act, did you?" Trina asked.

"He would have admitted he stole it before you stomped on the backpack," I said.

"I know I would have if you were gonna stomp on *my* game," Remi added.

Her shoulders slumped as the truth settled in. Her bike was gone and so was our only lead. Remi patted her back to console her. My stomach churned and I wanted to throw up, but I pushed the "down" button on my vomit elevator.

"What do we do now?" Remi asked.

The mystery was starting to grow. First Trina's bike was stolen. Now Eric's game was missing. We were dealing with more than a simple thief.

I told my friends my theory. "I think a kleptomaniac is taking everything."

"A clip toe what?" Remi said.

"*Hel-lo*, kleptomaniac," Trina said. "A crazy thief."

She had it right. I remembered the definition by breaking the word in two. On a television cop show, I had heard the police actors call a thief "Klepto."

Maniac reminded me of Mr. E and the Asylum House. A "kleptomaniac" was a crazy person who couldn't stop stealing.

The school bell rang, signalling the end of lunch hour. Very few of the students headed straight into the building. Mr. E's talk about Pavlov's dogs had worked on everyone.

"Maybe this kelp-toe-maniac can steal my homework," Remi said.

"Klep, not kelp," I said.

"It's not a guy who steals seaweed," Trina said, snickering.

"I don't have to help, you know," Remi said.

"Don't you mean kelp?" she teased. "Silly."

She smacked him on the shoulder. He blushed. An insult and a slap on the arm. Things were getting serious between the two of them.

"We have to make a list," I said, cutting off the lovebird chatter and pulling out my detective's notebook, "of people in the school who might be kleptomaniacs."

Remi blurted, "Jacques and Jean. Definitely."

The Boissonault brothers. Twin towers of trouble. Everyone was afraid of getting on the wrong side of the French fiends. I wanted to say they were the kind of guys who grabbed what they wanted rather than stole, but I jotted their names in the notebook.

Trina declared, "Samantha McNally is my main suspect."

They were best friends before the summer holidays. Inseparable like spit sisters, except they swapped clothes instead of saliva. They were never apart before, but something must have happened over the summer.

"I thought you two were friends," Remi said. "She didn't invite me to her pool party."

"That doesn't make her a thief," I said.

"Put her on the list."

I wrote Samantha's name in the notebook.

"Who else?" Remi asked.

Silence. We had run out of suspects. We agreed to follow everyone after school. Remi headed to the French side of the building while I walked with Trina to the English side.

"Let me use your notebook," she said. "I'll write down everything Samantha does."

"I'll give you your own notebook. I have a spare book in my locker," I said.

In the hall, I dialled my lock combination. The lock was sticky, but after a few pulls, it opened. When I looked inside the locker, however, I noticed something was wrong. My stuff had been rearranged. Textbooks were opened and my pencil case was spilled open. My lime-green scribbler, the one with all my secret notes and doodles of Toronto Maple Leafs emblems and Trina hearts, was missing.

Seven

I was sure I'd fastened my lock and checked it twice. How could anyone get into my locker without knowing the combination? I smacked my head, punishing myself for failing to check the lock three times.

"Are you sure your notebook isn't in there?" Trina asked. "Let me look."

The last thing I wanted was for anyone, especially Trina, to see my secret love doodles. I waved her off.

"Who has the lockers beside you? Maybe one of them broke in."

"Zack is here," I said, tapping the locker to the right of me.

The kids nicknamed him the Lint, because he was always trying to hang out with the popular boys, who I nicknamed the Hoppers, because they spent so much time practising bunny hops on their mountain bikes in the parking lot. They'd try to shake him off, but he stuck to them like lint. I could imagine Zack using the bike and video game to try to score points to get some face time with the Hoppers.

"I think we should put him on the list," I suggested.

"Who's on the other side?"

"Samantha."

Trina raised an eyebrow. I could pretty well guess what she was thinking.

"We'd better get to class," I said. "Maybe we'll catch the kleptomaniac with the book in his desk."

"Or *her* desk."

In the classroom kids were clustered in small groups. Our teacher wasn't there, which meant no one was in charge and we could act like it was recess inside the school. The athletic kids arm wrestled each other. A couple of kids sat quietly at their desks reading. A few girls tried to feed the class hamster. The Hoppers talked near Mr. E's desk while Zack hovered nearby.

Trina locked on to Samantha, who was taking charge of feeding the hamster. She adjusted her gold glasses and straightened her bright blue blouse, which looked exactly like the blouse Trina wore yesterday. She had stolen Trina's fashion sense.

"I'll talk to her," she said. "See if you can get anything out of Zack."

I headed toward the Lint, who sat on the edge of Mr. E's desk, trying to join a conversation about *Robot Rampage.*

"I like Rocky Robot," he said, trying to jump into the conversation. "He's going to be the champion."

None of the Hoppers answered him. They moved away from the teacher's desk and continued talking about other robots and their weapons of metal destruction. The Lint tried to follow them, but I cut him off.

"I like Rocky Robot, too," I lied. If I could get on his good side, he might slip up and give me some vital information.

"Yeah, he's really cool, because he has mallets for arms and he can bonk the other robots on the head and smash them flat like pancakes. Sometimes I wish I had mallets for arms."

"Cool," I said.

"I'd be like smash, smash, smash, smash."

Zack swung his arms up and down like mallets and accidentally knocked over Mr. E's space shuttle model, which fell into his half-opened desk drawer.

"I'll get it," I said, reaching into the drawer.

As I picked up the model I noticed a smooth black pencil case inside the drawer.

"What are you doing?" Mr. E shouted from behind me.

I froze with my hand on the model. Zack pointed at me.

"He did it."

I turned around, but Mr. E wasn't looking at me. He was talking to Ida in the doorway. She was holding a chocolate bar.

"You can't eat candy any time you feel like it," he said. "Not when class is about to start."

"Why not?" she asked.

"When you're in this class, you live by my rules."

"Maybe I don't want to be in your class any more."

She was going to be in a world of trouble for talking back to the teacher, but Mr. E did nothing except scratch his beard.

"You don't have a choice," he said. "You have to be careful. Of all people, you should know better."

She tossed the chocolate bar at him and stomped to her desk, pulling up the collar of her leather jacket. Mr. E watched her go and shook his head. No detention. No punishment. No lecture. I wondered if he was scared of Ida. I certainly was.

Our teacher barked at everyone, "Get to your desks."

Everyone scrambled to their seats. Mr. E took a deep breath and paced around the front of the classroom. His white hair bounced up and down as he walked. He took a few deep breaths, closed his eyes for a second and waited.

Finally, he opened his eyes and spoke. "Who is the strongest student in the whole school?"

Every Hopper shot his hand up, along with most of the guys in class. I kept my hand down. Trina raised her hand and waved, catching Mr. E's attention.

"Trina Brewster, do you think you're stronger than these strapping young gentlemen?" He waved at the eager boys stretching their hands up to the ceiling.

"Stronger smelling, maybe," Eric joked.

"*Hel-lo*, Mr. E wasn't talking to you."

"She's right, Eric. You should wait until I ask you to speak before you say anything."

"Sorry."

Weird. Mr. E lectured Eric for speaking out of turn, but Ida got away with talking back. I noted this in my detective's notebook. Why didn't the thief take this book instead of my secret green scribbler?

Mr. E held up two small red and white bars that looked like packs of gum.

"This will separate the strong from the weak. All you have to do is hold the two bars together so that their ends touch. Who wants to test their strength?"

"Me," Eric said, getting up from his seat. He flexed his biceps like a wrestler about to step into the ring.

Mr. E handed him the bars and Eric moved the red ends together, but the bars did not touch. His eyes widened with surprise, but he wasn't about to give up. He set his feet wider, rolled his shoulders, and took a deep breath. Then he pushed the red ends of the bars together. Again, they wouldn't meet. Everyone started to laugh.

Eric said, "Shut up. I'm concentrating."

He tried again and failed. The kids laughed even louder.

Mr. E waved everyone to be quiet as he took the bars away from the grunting Eric. "That's enough. Who's next?"

The Hoppers did not raise their hands. No one was eager to look like a wimp. But Trina wasn't scared. She raised her hand.

Mr. E smiled and handed the bars to her. Instead of pushing the red ends together, she flipped the bars around and tried to push the white ends together.

"It's a trick," she explained. "But I figured it out."

She pushed the bars together, but they didn't touch. She couldn't make the white ends touch no matter how hard she pushed. The bars slipped past each other, but the ends never touched.

Everyone laughed. She turned beet red. She handed the bars back to Mr. E and joined Eric on the side.

"Who else wants to try?"

Judging by how everyone was staring down at their desks, I imagined that Mr. E would have had better luck asking for volunteers to clean out the hamster cage.

"No one? That's okay. You were half right about this being a trick, Trina." He flipped *one* of the bars and pushed the red end toward the white end. The bars clicked together. He let go of one bar and the two magnets held together.

"How did you do that?" Samantha asked. "That's so cool."

"What are they?" Zack asked, his eyes wide with curiosity.

Mr. E pulled the magnets apart. "Have you ever heard the saying 'opposites attract'?"

Samantha put her hand up. "That's about people falling in love."

The boys snickered.

She continued, "My mom says that two people who have nothing in common will usually end up together. She said that's why my aunt and uncle broke up. It was because they were too alike. Dad said they broke up because Uncle Simon had a wandering eye. Do you know what that means?"

"Let's stick with your mom's explanation. If magnets are too much the same, they won't like each other. But if they're opposites, they go together just like this."

Mr. E snapped the magnets together again.

"But they look exactly alike," Zack pointed out.

"You're right. But here's the trick. Every magnet has a positive pole, which some people call the south pole." He tapped the red end of one magnet. "And every magnet also has a negative pole. What do you think it's called?"

"North pole?" I answered.

Mr. E tapped the magnet's white end. "Very good, Marty. Now science lovers, and that means you too

Eric, you're going to do some magnet magic. I want you to make a magnet float in mid-air."

"This isn't Hogwarts," Eric joked. "We're not wizards."

Our teacher smiled. "Good thing for you, or else I'd turn you into a moth."

Everyone laughed. Mr. E stepped behind his desk and pulled out a box of supplies. He held up a Styrofoam board and some pencils.

"You have to use your science minds today. All you have are two magnets, this Styrofoam board and four pencils. That's all you need to make a magnet float in the air. It's pretty simple to figure out, but if you have trouble here's a clue. Think about the bull riders at the Rainmaker Rodeo. If you remember where they start, you'll be able to make the magnets float. Break into groups of four."

Trina got up, grabbed my wrist and led me toward Samantha. This was our chance to get close to the prime suspect. Ida shambled over and made up the last of the foursome. Trina took charge. She set the Styrofoam board on top of her desk.

Samantha suggested, "Maybe we should put it upside down in case Mr. E put magnets on the one side."

"No," Trina barked. "Leave the board the way it is. Marty, go sharpen the pencils. I know exactly what to do."

I wondered if she wanted to make up for the fact that she hadn't figured out the magnet trick earlier. As I walked past the station beside us, Zack jammed the eraser end of a pencil up his nose. His Hopper team members moved away as he reached for a second pencil.

"Take the pencil out of your nose," Mr. E ordered Zack.

"I think it's stuck."

"Come to my desk."

Everyone tried to make the magnets float. Some tried to jam the magnets into the Styrofoam boards. Hannah stacked one of the magnets on a teeter-totter of pencils. She launched it into the air. No one had any luck keeping the magnets afloat. I headed back to my station with the sharpened pencils. Ida was the centre of attention in our group. She held one of the magnets over Samantha's watch.

"That's a fluke," Samantha said.

"Hold still," Ida ordered.

Samantha tried to pull her arm away, but Ida held on to her by the sleeve of her blue blouse.

"What's going on?" I asked.

Trina looked up at me. "Look at what the magnet is doing to Samantha's watch."

Under the glass face, the watch's second hand jittered backwards and forwards.

"Can a magnet screw up other things?" I asked.

"If it's powerful enough, it probably could," Trina said.

Samantha piped up. "But the thing has to be metal."

"How do you know?" Trina asked.

Samantha grabbed the magnet from Ida and placed it on her coiled scribbler. The magnet didn't stick to the cover, until she slid it across to the metal coil. Then it clicked and didn't budge.

"Any idea how to make the magnet float?" Ida said, now bored.

"Can I have the magnet?" I asked.

She handed it over, while I picked the other one up from the desk. I laid them both on top of the white board along with the four newly sharpened pencils. I thought about Mr. E's clue. I remembered watching bull riders at the Rainmaker Rodeo in St. Albert. The cowboy climbed on the back of a bull inside a tiny corral, and he hung on until the gate opened and the bucking bull blasted out of the cramped wooden pen.

"I think I know how to do it," I said.

I picked up a pencil and stabbed it into the white board. Then, stabbing in the other three pencils, I made my own magnet corral. Once I'd built my fence, I placed one magnet between the pencil fence posts. The fit was tight and I had to squeeze the magnets between the pencils.

"That's it?" Ida said, sneering. "I could have done that."

Trina picked up the other magnet. "I think I know what's next."

Beside her, Samantha kept checking her watch. "I think my watch is running backwards now."

Trina lowered the magnet toward the other bar, matching up colour to colour so that the red ends and the white ends were aligned. About halfway into the pencil corral, she stopped. She pulled her hand away and the top magnet floated in mid air just a hair above the bottom one, like a rider about to be bucked off his bull. I clapped. Samantha cheered. Ida yawned.

Mr. E walked to our station, wiping his fingers with a tissue – probably getting rid of Zack's booger. "Excellent job. I have four budding scientists," he said.

"Whoopee," Ida said, but it didn't sound like she meant it. "Aren't we so brilliant."

"Outside, young lady. We need to talk. Right now."

Everyone went "oooo," as Mr. E escorted Ida outside the classroom. She must have pushed our teacher too far.

Meanwhile, Samantha kept checking her watch. I looked at the floating magnet and the truth clicked into place like the two magnets from the earlier demonstration. I whispered in Trina's ear. "I think I know how the thief broke into my locker."

She looked at me, puzzled. "How?"

I held out the magnets.

EIGHT

Find the magnets, find the thief. But to be sure, I had to get more information about the thefts. Anyone could have grabbed Trina's bike off the street, but the thief broke into Eric's and my lockers. The search of my locker turned up no clues, which meant that we had to talk to Eric. If we helped him find his video game, I was sure that we'd find the other loot. At recess, I shared my theory with my detective partners.

Trina shook her head. "Why should we help Eric?"

Remi nodded. "You have to admit, Marty, the guy hasn't been the nicest to you. Why bother?"

All the times Eric gave me an atomic wedgie jumped to mind. Out of habit, I adjusted my underwear. But if my enemy held the key to finding the thief, I was willing to forget about the bunched-up underwear. "He might give us a clue about the thief."

"Samantha stole everything," Trina said. "She's got a grudge against me. And Eric didn't invite her to his birthday party last year, so I think she doesn't like him either."

Remi leaned closer to her. "She's right, Marty."

"She's got no proof."

"Neither do you," she said.

"I will after I talk to Eric."

"You can play silly games if you want. I'm watching Samantha." Trina walked away.

"It wasn't that long ago she was sure Eric was the thief," I said. "She'll come around. Are you going to help?"

"Sorry, Marty," Remi said. He started after her.

"Where are you going?"

"I gotta find out if she like-*likes* me or not. Maybe she'll drop a hint when we're talking about the case."

"Why don't you just ask her?" I suggested.

"Are you nuts?" Remi asked. "I want to know if she like-*likes* me, but I don't want her to know that I like-*like* her until I know for sure that she like-*likes* me first."

He made sense. I'd never tell anyone my feelings until I knew how they felt, but it could take forever before she said anything.

"Remi, why don't you give her a note from a secret admirer, and then ask her who she hopes the note is from?"

"Hey, not a bad idea. Gimme some paper."

I handed him a sheet of paper.

"And a pencil."

I gave him a pencil.

"Can you write the note? She might recognize my handwriting."

The things I did for my friend! I wrote:

My heart beats faster
When you're around
You've stolen my heart
I'm your lovesick hound

I promised Remi I'd help him, but I didn't think that promise meant having to use my secret feelings to help him win Trina's heart. I felt like I was the big-nosed hero in the DVD that my parents watched last year. Cyrano helped his best friend flirt with a beautiful woman, but Cyrano also loved her. His messages of love came straight from his heart, even though the words came out of his friend's mouth.

He scanned my love note.

"Perfect," he said. "You should be a writer. I'll slip this in her backpack. You talk to Eric."

My friend jogged away, leaving me alone. The weird flutter in my stomach grew stronger. Maybe I should have joined them to keep him from planting the note. What would Cyrano do? In the movie, he helped his friend. I let Remi go.

After school, I waited by Eric's locker for him. As usual, he was in the detention room for one of his many bone-headed pranks. Today he'd stuffed paper towels in all the boys' toilets so they overflowed. I only knew this because I had to go to the bathroom really badly right after he pulled the prank, and I ended up using the girls' washroom.

Finally, Eric came out of the detention room. He pushed me out of the way and started to dial the combination on his lock.

"I want to help you find your game, Eric."

He opened his locker. "Why do you want to help me?"

"Whoever took your game is probably the same person who stole Trina's bike."

"Why do you care so much?"

"Someone broke into my locker," I said. "It might be the same person."

"No way. What did they take?"

"My green scribbler."

Eric's face twisted up like I'd told him I liked to wear pink slippers and a tutu.

"It had a lot of important information inside," I explained.

"Ooo, how are you going to live without your notes on long division?"

"Do you want your game back or not?" I asked.

He reluctantly nodded and told me everything.

Eric Johnson's Witness Statement

As Recorded by Detective Marty Chan

— victim (Eric Johnson) was minding his own business trying to get a high score on Ridge Racer when Mr. E told him to put the game away.

— victim reported Mr. E saying that people can have more fun making games than playing them. The victim is not sure what Mr. E said next because he was too busy playing the game.

— Mr. E took the game away from the victim. Teacher was going to put the game in his desk drawer, victim promised he would put it in his locker. Victim thought his locker was safer, plus he thought he could play another game if he walked really slowly.

— victim did not get high score by the time he reached the locker. No one was in the hallway when he put away the game.

— victim swears that no one at school knows his combination. The victim also swears that whoever stole his game is going to be in for the mother of all atomic wedgies.

— I asked victim for a list of people who might have a grudge against him.

People who might have a problem with
Eric Johnson

— Trina
— Principal Henday
— Mr. E
— Samantha
— His mom
— His dad
— His big brother
— Hannah
— Zack

— The chess club
— Marty
— The Hoppers
— All the grade threes
— All the grade fours . . .

People who <u>don't</u> have a problem with
Eric Johnson

— His grandma (the oldest driver in the world) and
his grandpa

After the interview, I had to inspect the crime scene. I pulled a freezer bag out of my backpack and donned a pair of mittens. Then I handed Eric a roll of masking tape to mark off the crime scene area.

"You take things seriously," he said.

I removed Eric's cracked magnifying glass from my backpack.

"Is that my magnifying glass?" he asked.

"The one you were using to burn ants?" I said.

"Uh . . . never mind."

"Move back."

He stepped outside of the crime scene tape line as I approached the locker. A funky smell came from a paper bag at the top of a pile of books. Inside the bag were a mouldy sandwich and a peach that had gone bad. The smell punched up my nose and made me want to throw up. I closed the bag, took it out and placed it on the floor. Next, I removed Eric's books. All the textbooks looked brand new, as if they'd never been opened. The scribblers were still wrapped in plastic. The pencil crayons were as blunt as chopsticks. This was the locker of a guy who did *not* care about school. Once the locker was empty, I started to examine the door and the combination lock for fingerprints.

Taking a cue from the police shows I saw on TV, I pulled a thick brush and circular container out of my backpack. I cracked the lid, dipped the brush into the puck-shaped container and dusted the locker door with flour. Most of the white stuff slid off the metal and landed on Eric's books.

"You're making a mess," he shouted.

"I'm dusting for fingerprints."

I brushed flour on the sides of the combination lock. None of it stuck. My fingerprint plan was failing. Maybe not everything on TV worked in real life.

"Are you punking me?"

I ignored Eric and continued dusting, coating the entire locker with flour. I blew the flour off the metal, expecting to see fingerprint smudges. Instead, I got a nose full of flour.

"Achoo!" I backed up and blew some more, but there were no fingerprints. A ridge of flour formed on the bottom lip of the locker. I swept it away and caught my mitten on something sharp.

"You're gonna clean this up, right?"

"In a minute," I said.

Jutting out of the bottom lip of the locker was a broken hairpin. The zig-zag ridges were covered with flour, and one end looked like it had been filed down to be very thin. I showed Eric the hairpin.

"Is this yours?"

He squinted at the hairpin and shook his head. "Do I look like a girl?"

I pulled a sandwich bag from my backpack, flapped it open, and placed the hairpin inside. Maybe in the rush to steal the game, the thief had dropped the hairpin. I stepped over the mountain of junk in front of the locker.

"I'm done." I walked away.

Behind me, Eric yelled, "Whoa! You're not done until you clean up this mess."

I tidied up everything but the funky lunch bag and headed back to my locker. I dialled my combination as I tried to piece together how a magnet, a hairpin, a bike, a video game player and my scribbler fit together. There had to be a connection between all these things, but what was it?

I opened my locker: there sat Eric's stolen video game.

NINE

The thief was trying to frame me for stealing Eric's video game!

What was I going to do with the stolen game? No way could I give it back to Eric. This was what the thief wanted. He needed a fall guy to take the blame. Remi would have called this clever move the Fart Finger. Whenever someone smelled a fart and asked who cut the cheese, fingers would point in all directions like exploding porcupine quills. Everyone avoided the guy who received the most finger points. I did not want to be that guy, so I had to keep the video game under wraps.

I opened my backpack so I could slide the game inside, but just as I reached into my locker, I heard Mr. E clear his throat. He had sidled up beside me. I spun around and closed the locker.

"Marty, what are you still doing here?" he asked.

My stomach lurched as if I'd downed an entire bottle of foul-tasting cough syrup. I had to keep my teacher from looking inside the locker.

"I forgot my homework," I lied.

"Why are you sweating?"

"It's hot in here."

"Are you sure? I was thinking it might be because you're hiding something."

I froze. Had Mr. E seen the game? I shook my head.

"Marty, do you know Erwin Schrödinger?"

"Is he the new janitor?"

He shook his head. "He was a very clever scientist who had this strange idea about a cat and a paradox. Do you know what a paradox is, Marty?"

I fumbled with the word in my mind. "Para" could mean two of something, like a *pair*. But two of what? The last part of the word sounded like docks. Two docks? Two places to park boats? But only one boat. I took a stab at the answer. "It's when you have two things, but you only need one."

He smiled. "Close. It's when two opposite things are true, but they can't be true at the same time. Erwin said that if he had a cat in a box with a radio-active element, the cat would die, but you'd never know when it died until you opened the box. He said the cat in the box was always going to be dead and alive at the same time, and the only time it would be one or the other was when you opened the box. Do you understand?"

I didn't, but I nodded. If I gave Mr. E what he wanted, he might walk away. No such luck.

"You say your homework is in your locker, and it might be homework or it might be something else. The only way I'm going to know for sure what's inside is to open the door and look."

I wished Remi was with me now so he could help me, but he was probably kissing Trina behind the shed. The only way I'd know for sure was if I looked behind the shed. Now I knew what paradox meant – things no one wanted to see.

My teacher reached into his jacket pocket. "There are two kinds of people in this world, Marty. Troublemakers and trouble-takers. I'm sure you're familiar with the first kind."

I shook my head.

He cocked his head to one side. "Are you sure?"

Out of his pocket he pulled the other half of the mangled hockey puck. My teacher, the maniac, knew I was spying on him. I looked down at my feet.

"I thought so," Mr. E said, grinning. "Personally, I like trouble-takers, because they take the troubles away from others."

He was building a strong case against me, and all the proof he needed sat inside my locker. Only one way out.

"Someone stole my scribbler," I said.

He raised an eyebrow.

"They broke into my locker. I think the thief must have used magnets to mess up my lock."

My teacher shook his head. "Magnets don't affect combination locks. The only way you can get into a lock is to use a pick. Something sharp and flat."

"You mean like what I found stuck in Eric's locker?" I said, holding up the bag containing the hairpin. "Ask him. He'll tell you I found it there."

He stiffened. "Why didn't you report this earlier, Marty?"

"I wanted to be sure I had some proof," I said.

"Hold on, that doesn't explain what's in your locker. What's in there?"

I had to give Mr. E a reason to look somewhere else. "Uh . . . my underwear. I kind of had an accident at lunch."

He stepped back. "What kind of accident?"

"The kind that everyone laughs at," I said.

"Number one or number two?"

"One," I said. "I was waiting until everyone left so I could take the underwear home without anyone making fun of me. I was really thirsty in the morning and I had three juice boxes and I made at least ten trips to the water fountain. And then one of the grade six boys said if I had to pee, the best thing to do was squeeze my stomach and think about rain. It didn't work."

"Nice try. Open the locker."

Suddenly, a voice shouted, "It's time! Let's get this over with."

Ida stood in the doorway to the classroom playing with her wristband. Mr. E turned around.

"In a minute."

"I'll get it next time if you're busy," she yelled.

"No. We'll do it now." He waved at me. "Go home, Marty."

He walked briskly back to his classroom and ushered Ida through the doorway. "Ida, what did I tell you about the wristband?"

"It's not hurting anyone," she said.

He closed the door behind them, muting the rest of their conversation. Ida had saved me. I opened the locker and stuffed Eric's game into my backpack.

What power did Ida have over our teacher that she could say it was "time" and he'd go running? The list of mysteries to solve kept growing. As I closed my backpack, the pieces of the puzzle started to lock together like the zipper's metal teeth.

Trina's bike had disappeared beside his house. Eric's game disappeared after Mr. E had talked about it. And my teacher had conveniently shown up at my locker just as I found the stolen game. He showed me the other half of the mangled puck, which meant he knew Remi and I were staking out his house. We had dismissed him as a suspect earlier because he was a teacher, but what a perfect cover for a thief. Now Mr. E was pointing the fart finger right at me. Who better to blame for the thefts than the guy trying to catch the thief?

The only way to save myself and to solve the crime was to find the bike, and the only place Mr. E could have hidden the bike was inside his house. One way or another, I had to see what was inside the Asylum House.

TEN

Getting into Mr. E's house was impossible because when we were out of school, so was our teacher. Somehow, I had to get *out* of school and keep him *in* school. To do that, I needed help.

The next morning, I told Trina and Remi about my run-in with Mr. E and my plan to get into his house to look for her bike. They didn't believe me at first, but when I showed them the stolen video game and the hairpin lock pick, they changed their tune.

"I'll help you look," Remi offered.

"Thanks. We need someone to keep Mr. E at school." I looked at Trina.

"No way," she said. "Why me?"

He explained, "He's not my teacher, so I can't make him stay."

"Marty can do it."

He started to waffle. "Maybe Trina's right. She can run faster than both of us. Plus, she knows what her bike looks like."

"No," I said. I didn't want to deal with another paradox, wondering if they were holding hands or not in Mr. E's yard. I wanted the old detective duo back together again. Frank and Joe Hardy. Batman and Robin. Harry Potter and Ron Weasley.

She crossed her arms. "Well, I'm not going to help unless I get to go."

She could be so stubborn. "Okay, you can go, but if the police catch you, I hope you have a good story," I said.

"The police . . . " Trina bit her lower lip.

Remi shot me a dirty look. I'd just figured out how to solve a paradox. Don't put the cat in the box and don't let Trina and Remi go alone.

"I'm sure the cops won't come."

"Remi's probably right. You should be *mostly* safe." I sensed she didn't want to get in trouble.

She fidgeted from one foot to the other. Remi smacked me on the back of the head. I refused to back off. I was going to try to keep my promise to help him impress Trina, but I wasn't going to lose my best friend doing it.

"Do you still want to go?" he asked.

She shook her head. "I'll be the school decoy."

Remi glared at me. He'd have to find another way to score points with Trina.

I shrugged. "It's what she wants."

At the end of the school day, I glanced up at the clock. Almost time for dismissal. Time to put the plan into action. I tapped Trina's back with the eraser end of my pencil but she didn't budge.

I scribbled a note — "Do it." — and passed it to her.

She passed the note back to me. She had scribbled on the back; "I don't want to get in trouble."

I crossed out her message and wrote over it: "If *I* do it, he'll know something's up."

I tossed the note over her shoulder, but it fell into her open backpack on the floor. Trina reached into her backpack for the note. She pulled out *two* notes. She read both and sat still for what seemed like forever.

She spun around in her desk and held up the love note that I had written to help Remi win her heart. "Lovesick hound? Who wrote this poem?"

My hands started to sweat. "Maybe you have a secret admirer," I said.

"This is *your* handwriting." She held up both notes.

She was a better detective than me. I should have told her that the poem was from Remi and I was just the messenger. Instead, I broke a promise to my best friend.

"Um, maybe."

I couldn't figure out from Trina's expression if she'd just sucked on a lemon or if she'd tasted a sweet orange. I hoped she found the note sweet.

Mr. E yelled from the front of the class, "What's in your hand Trina? Are you passing notes?"

She stuffed the notes into her mouth and chewed.

"Spit that out," Mr. E ordered.

She stood up.

Mr. E ordered, "Sit down, Trina."

Trina started to dance while she chewed the notes.

"This isn't funny."

She kept dancing.

"Enough."

She kept dancing after the bell rang. No one moved. They were no longer Pavlov's dogs. Now they were Trina's dogs. She jumped on her seat and shook her arms in the air while everyone gawked at her. I snuck out of my desk and headed out of the classroom. Just as I reached the doorway, I stopped and looked back at Trina. Our eyes met.

Did she like-*like* me? I'd crumble to pieces if she didn't. Give me a sign. Any kind of sign. She flashed a small smile. My heart swelled.

"Tap dance number!" she said. She tapped on the desk, while Mr. E tried to get her off the chair.

"You're getting detention for this."

I bounded down the hallway, thrilled that Trina might like-*like* me. I felt like I was running on air, but I crashed to the Earth when I ran into Remi.

"What are you smiling about, Marty?"

I tried to wipe the smile off, but it was like permanent felt marker across my face. "Trina's dancing looks hilarious," I lied.

"Can I see?"

I shook my head. "We better get to Mr. E's house."

At the Asylum House, we caught our breath. We didn't have much time, but now that I was at the house, I was afraid to go through with my plan. Remi approached the wooden gate at the side of Mr. E's house and peeked through the slats. I joined him. The yard was full of weird metal pieces and strange machines. I reached over the fence, pulled up the latch and swung the gate open.

"After you," I said.

"You first."

"You go," I prompted.

"It was your idea."

"We don't have all day," I said. Remi must have been just as scared as I was.

"Then hurry up."

I stepped into the yard. Remi followed. Mr. E had a junkyard where his lawn should have been. Gutted refrigerators and stripped-down car engines filled the yard, along with other bits of scrap metal. This was the yard of a mad scientist. In the middle of the yard, a heavy tarp covered something large. Before I could go over and check under the cover, Remi nudged me.

"Marty," he whispered. "Look over there. By the house."

Across the minefield of scrap metal, a collection of bicycle wheels hung off the porch. Some were mangled, others in perfect condition. Did Mr. E rip apart Trina's bike for some kind of experiment? We crept toward the bicycle graveyard, looking for anything that might look like Trina's mountain bike. All the tires were flat and the spokes were rusted.

"They're from older bikes. We're going to have to check out the house," I said.

"It's getting late. How long do you think Trina can stall?"

"I told her to give us at least half an hour. If her detention ended early, she was supposed to start disco dancing."

Remi grinned. "She must hate you."

Exactly the opposite, but I wasn't going to say anything. I just nodded as I crept on to the porch. The stairs groaned under my weight. I froze. I reminded myself that no one was around. I kept climbing to the front door. I was about to pull on the screen door handle when I felt a tap on my shoulder.

"Did Trina find the note in her backpack?"

"This isn't the best time to be asking that," I said.

"I'm wondering, that's all."

I grabbed the door handle.

"Well, did she say anything?" Remi asked.

"No," I said. Technically, I wasn't lying. She didn't *say* anything, but her tiny smile might as well have said "I love you forever and ever, Marty."

He fell silent. I pulled open the screen door and tested the doorknob. The house was locked. I pulled out the hairpin and magnet. One of these things had to help me open the door.

"This isn't a good sign, is it? I mean, she should have found the note by now. And if she has, then it means she's not interested in secret admirers."

I shrugged. "Maybe." Maybe not.

"I should just tell her how I feel. What do you think?"

"Bad idea," I said. "I think you have to play it cool."

I hated keeping him in the dark, but he wasn't ready to see the pair of love ducks that was Trina and me. I was also worried that he might say something that would change her mind about me. I was a terrible friend for thinking that.

"Let's find the bike first," I said. "Hold the magnet."

I tossed him the magnet so he could wave it around the lock, while I started to pick at the keyhole with the hairpin. I didn't know what I was doing with the hairpin, but at least it kept me busy and allowed me to avoid talking about the love poem.

The lock wouldn't open. I put the hairpin back in my pocket. I wished I could crawl inside the pocket with it and hide from Remi's questions.

He handed me the magnet. "What do we do now?"

I wasn't sure if he was talking about the door or about Trina. I pretended it was about the door.

"I don't know."

"You've got to promise me, Marty. Do whatever you can to make her like-*like* me."

I looked down at the junk in the yard for some way out of the hole that I'd dug. There was only one way to go. Dig the hole deeper.

"Sure," I lied.

"You're my best friend."

I didn't feel like a friend right now. "We'd better leave before Mr. E gets back."

"Yeah."

We headed off the porch. *Click. Clack. Click clack.* Someone was trying to unlatch the gate.

Remi looked at me, his eyes wide with panic. I pointed to the table in the middle of the yard. We sprinted toward the tarp-covered table, lifted the heavy cloth and ducked under the table. As we curled up under the table, I could hear someone walking through the yard. I peeked out from under the tarp, but the junk prevented me from seeing the person's face.

Remi whispered, "It's too soon for Mr. E to come home."

I agreed.

Crunch, crunch, crunch. The horrible truth started to sink in. The intruder was walking toward us. We inched backwards, but there was nowhere we could go. As long as we hid under the tarp we were safe. Hopefully, this was someone delivering flyers and he'd leave very soon.

Suddenly, the intruder grabbed the tarp and yanked it off the table.

Eleven

The tarp crumpled to the ground behind us. Cool fall air blew up my pant legs as I curled up into a ball and inched the tarp over Remi and me. I thought about the buzzing sound we'd heard just before the mangled hockey puck flew over the hedge. I didn't want the same thing to happen to us.

Remi wrapped himself tighter in the tarp. I peeked out from the folds. So far, the intruder had said nothing. Maybe he didn't see us. Until he said something, the best thing we could do was stay put. We waited for the man in the cotton pants to make the first move.

"Not bad, Eisenberg," said a nasally voice. This didn't sound like Mr. E, but he did sound serious, because he was using our teacher's last name.

I scanned the yard for someone else, but it seemed like Mr. Cotton Pants was talking to himself.

"But it lacks true imagination and creativity. Your inventions are so 1997. Still, let's say you had a little setback."

The screech of metal scraping against metal clawed at my ears. I covered them until the sound had faded. Suddenly, an electric buzz hummed through the air, followed by a scream. The man in the cotton pants jumped back from the table.

Remi poked his head out from the tarp; his hair was standing straight up. If I weren't so scared, I'd have laughed.

Suddenly, a different voice spoke. It sounded like a girl's voice, but computerized. "Please do not handle the merchandise, Davis."

Davis. The name sounded familiar.

Mr. Cotton Pants sounded less smug. "Voice recognition. Impressive for a prototype."

"May I suggest you steal your invention ideas from someone else? Have you tried visiting school science fairs? I think that is more your level."

"Let's see you laugh this off."

The electric hum grew louder and I could feel a static charge building in my hair. Mr. Cotton Pants stepped back. The hum faded.

"You can't hide your secrets forever."

"Thank you for visiting. Is there anything you'd like me to tell my creator?"

"Send him this message. He's never going to win."

The intruder stormed out of the yard, leaving us alone.

"Davis was the guy Mr. E thought we worked for," Remi said.

Of course. Why didn't I make the connection sooner? Remi was way better at remembering names than I was. I thought it might have something to do with the fact that he had to remember the names of his hockey team mates.

"Do you think it's safe yet?"

"Give it a couple more minutes," I said.

We watched the yard for any sign of Davis' return, but it looked like he was gone. We crawled out from under the tarp. On the table sat the top half of a robot. Its chest plate was opened, revealing a circuit board and multi-coloured wires. The metal arms looked like factory machines. At the end of the right arm was a metal claw, while the left arm ended in a buzz saw. Remi nudged me in the ribs.

"I think I know what destroyed the puck," he whispered.

I nodded, then I turned my attention to the robot's head. Brown hair cascaded over the robot's face. It looked almost real. I had to see the thing's face. I swept the hair away and stepped back.

The robot was Ida.

TWELVE

E erie didn't quite sum up what I was feeling. *Freaktastic* was getting closer to how it felt to be looking at the human head of Ida on half a robot. Her eyes were closed. Remi touched her cheek. Her eyelids fluttered for a second, but her eyes stayed closed.

"It's so real," he reported. "Feel it. Almost human."

My mind went wild with theories about why Mr. E would build a human-looking robot. I wondered how many of the parts were machine and how much was flesh and blood. I shuddered to think what Mr. E used for spare parts.

"Touch it," Remi said.

Slowly, I reached for the robot's cheek.

Suddenly her eyes popped wide open. "Please do not handle the merchandise, Davis," she ordered. She even sounded like Ida.

"I'm not Davis," I said.

She blinked twice. "May I suggest you steal your invention ideas from someone else? Have you tried visiting school science fairs? I think that is more your level."

Her lips moved out of sync with her words. It was like watching an old martial arts movie where the actors' voices were dubbed with actors who had British accents. Except this was no movie.

Remi whispered, "She's just repeating herself."

I nodded. "But isn't this the part when she zapped Davis?"

"Duck!"

I did, but nothing happened.

"Why didn't she zap us?" he asked.

"Do you remember, he was trying to open her up? Maybe she's got some kind of self-defence system."

"Let's not touch her," he said, eying the buzz-saw hand.

"Good idea."

"We're not going to touch you," Remi shouted at the robot. "Please don't zap us."

"Thank you for visiting. Is there anything you'd like me to tell my creator?"

A few seconds passed. Then the Ida robot shut her eyes and powered down. This must have been some kind of pre-recorded message.

"Cool. Let's make her do it again," he said, touching her cheek.

Her eyes opened, but instead of the blue eyes of earlier, they glowed red. This was not good.

"Intruder alert. Intruder alert. Intruder alert." she wailed, as her head lifted five inches into the air, revealing an iron rod neck. The robot head spun around again and again, the eyes flashing at us like laser beams.

"Run!" I yelled.

We scrambled over the junk in the yard and headed out. We sprinted down the alley. I didn't even bother looking back, afraid the robot would explode and wipe out the entire town of Bouvier. About two blocks away the sounds faded out. We slowed down to catch our breath.

"What do you think your teacher is doing with that robot?" he asked. "And why does it look like the girl from your class?"

I shook my head, still panting. "I don't know, but it looks like we have to keep a closer watch on Ida."

The next day we launched Operation Ida: Known Better. Remi agreed to take the first shift spying on Ida. She was playing tag with some girls, so it wouldn't be hard to keep an eye on her. Remi wanted to team up with Trina.

"No, let's leave her out of this until we know a little more," I said. The last thing I wanted was for Remi to find out the truth.

"She'll want to know what we found out yesterday," Remi said. "And it'll give me a great reason to talk to her."

"Let me be the messenger, Remi," I offered, remembering the Cyrano movie. "I'll find out what she said and report back."

"Good idea. You're a great friend."

I wished he'd stop saying that. I felt bad enough already.

"I want you to tell me word for word everything she says. Everything," he called after me.

Trina was hiding in the bushes within earshot of Samantha and some grade five girls. I waited until the coast was clear and then slid into the bushes behind her. Her hair was damp. I took a whiff. Ah, strawberry shampoo. I tapped her on the shoulder.

She turned and flashed me a terrific smile that made me feel about two feet taller, but also turned my tongue into a salty pretzel.

"Um . . . er . . . ah . . . hi." That sounded so much better in my head.

Trina said nothing, looking into my eyes. Finally, she spoke. "No one ever gave me a poem before. It was really sweet. You're such a romantic."

She took my hand in hers. I felt ten feet tall and my pretzel tongue was getting soggy. I mumbled something that might have sounded like thanks.

"But . . . " she said.

I started to shrink but my tongue still felt like a pretzel. "Oh?"

"But should we tell Remi?"

My hand felt clammy against hers. "Why?"

She peeked through the bushes at the schoolyard. Remi was strolling around Ida, pretending not to look our way. Trina pulled me away from the bushes so no one in the yard could see us.

"I think he has a crush on me too. He's always asking me what I like and then he says he likes it too. And he keeps trying to smell my hair. It's kind of weird. Don't you think?"

"Sort of," I said.

"Anyway, I don't want to wreck your friendship. I think *you* should tell Remi about us. I don't want him to find out from someone else."

Telling him was the worst thing to do, but Trina didn't know about my promise. I also didn't want her to stop like-liking me.

"Good idea. I'll tell him. Please don't say anything to him until I tell you it's okay."

She agreed. "So, what did you find at Mr. E's house?"

"No bike, but we found a robot," I said.

She scrunched up her face, puzzled.

"Come on. Remi will fill you in."

We walked over to Remi, who was still watching Ida. He tried not to act weird around Trina and Trina pretended not to act weird around him. He told her everything about Mr. E's robot and Davis' visit. When he was done, she said nothing. She just punched my arm, hard.

"Ow. What was that for?" I rubbed my arm.

"That's for wasting my time. What do robots have to do with my bike?"

I stepped out of punching range.

Remi suggested, "Maybe Mr. E needs your bike for robot parts. Do you like robots, Trina?"

"No."

"Me neither."

I shushed them both as a squealing Ida ran past us, avoiding a tag. "The only thing I don't get is why he made the robot look like her."

"Maybe he wants to replace Ida so he has a student who isn't always talking back to him," he joked.

I laughed. Trina did not.

"When I was in detention," she said, "Ida hung around, even though she wasn't in trouble. She was telling Mr. E something about time. It's almost time. Or . . . it's time."

"She said the same thing the other day, too," I said.

"Hold on," Remi said. "What if Ida is also a robot?"

She looked at him like he had grown a third eye in the middle of his forehead. I shook my head at her. She said nothing.

"I know it sounds weird," he continued, "but we saw the robot in Mr. E's yard. It looked just like the girl in your class."

Why couldn't Mr. E have built a robot Ida already? Maybe there never was a human Ida, and this robot was some twisted science experiment. After all, the robot in the yard looked so life-like, except for the

128

weird buzz saw hand and all the wiring and green circuit boards where her heart should have been.

"You know when Ida talked about it being *time*, it was like she needed something from Mr. E. What does a robot need?" I asked.

"Electricity," Remi blurted out. "Her batteries needed a recharge."

"You can't be serious," Trina said.

"Maybe she's right," my friend said, backing off his original theory.

Her face half-sneered and half-grimaced. "You don't have to agree with everything I say! What do *you* think?"

"I don't know. What do *you* think?" He looked at her with wide puppy eyes.

"Never mind."

I jumped in. "Let's find out for sure."

"Maybe we can knock on her head and see if it's made of metal," she said, sneering.

Ida was still playing tag. If she kept running like that she'd probably burn out her batteries and need a recharge soon.

Trina noted, "The weird thing was Mr. E took out this black case from his desk after Ida said it was time."

That had to be the thin pencil case I had seen earlier.

"He told the rest of us to behave and then he took Ida out of the room. A few minutes later, Mr. E came back to the classroom with the case."

"But not Ida?" I asked.

"Nope. I don't know where she went."

"I bet he plugged her into a wall socket to recharge," Remi said.

"*Hel-lo . . .* "

I nudged Trina in the side before she could finish her thought. Part of me believed his story, but another part wanted to agree with Trina. I felt like I didn't know where to put my feet. It was like the time my dad said there wasn't a Santa Claus. Dad said that he was the one who bought all the presents and I should be thanking him and not Santa. I wanted to tell Dad he was wrong, but I couldn't help but think that if Dad *was* Santa, it would explain why I never got the toys I wanted for Christmas. But right now, I didn't have time to figure out who was right and who was wrong. I had to make sure that Trina and Remi stayed friends.

"You might be right, Remi," I said. "What do you think, Trina?"

"Maybe."

He jumped up and down. "Hold on! Maybe *Ida's* the one who stole your bike."

She didn't answer. Her eyes darted back and forth and all around. This was her thinking look. It was like her eyes were echoing what was going on in her head as she was playing mental whack-a-mole with all the bad ideas until only one good idea popped up. Trina might not have believed that Ida was a robot, but the idea that Ida stole her bike was something she could believe.

"Do you remember how the magnet screwed up Samantha's watch?" I asked. "Do you think it could do the same thing to a robot?"

"I don't know," Trina answered. "Too bad we don't have a magnet."

Remi pulled a magnet out of his pocket. "You mean this?"

THIRTEEN

At recess, Trina and I waited in the hallway until everyone cleared out of the classroom. Mr. E took forever to put on his orange safety vest, but he finally got dressed and left the room.

I pretended to tie my shoes and Trina took her time putting on her jacket, while our teacher walked past us. As he headed down the hallway, Trina's arm brushed against mine. Goose pimples sprang up all along my arm.

Remi ran around the corner.

"No running, young man," Mr. E ordered.

Remi mumbled an apology and walked slowly toward us. I tried to flatten out the goose pimples on my arm as we watched our mad science teacher walk outside to supervise students in the schoolyard.

"Remi, you watch the main door. Signal Trina if anyone's coming back in. Trina, you signal me if you see his signal."

"Okay," he said. "The signal is this." He made an air heart with his two fingers.

She bit her lip and nodded. "I'll whistle when I see the apple shape."

"It's not an apple, it's a —"

"Maybe you should both whistle," I said, cutting off my friend.

He nodded and headed down the hall while I crept back into the classroom. Trina grabbed my arm and whispered, "You didn't tell him, did you?"

"I didn't have the time. I'll do it later today. Promise." Another promise made in a rush. Next time, I should take more time to think through my promises.

Inside the classroom, I held the magnet to the back of the metal frame of Ida's seat. But the magnet didn't hold; it slipped down the metal bar and landed on the floor. I picked it up and tried again. The magnet wouldn't stick. Had it lost its attraction? Were people like magnets? Would Trina lose her attraction to me?

She poked her head in. "Hurry up, Marty. What's taking so long?"

"Another minute. Does Remi see anything?"

"No, but he keeps staring at me. It's starting to creep me out."

"I'm almost done."

She closed the door while I looked around for another way to attach the magnet to Ida's chair. On Mr. E's desk sat a tape dispenser. Perfect. I ran to his desk. As I tore off a strip of tape, however, I heard a faint whistle.

Trina called out, "Good morning, Principal Henday!"

I froze. If Mr. Henday caught me now, our plans would be ruined. I ducked behind Mr. E's desk and hoped my friends would distract the principal. His silhouette filled the frosted glass of the classroom door.

"Remi and I are playing air hockey," she said. "It's his turn to shoot. Don't worry, we're using an imaginary puck."

Silence. I held my breath.

Then, Mr. Henday spoke. "I'm looking for Mr. Eisenberg. Is he in the classroom?"

"No," Trina shouted. "He went outside."

I hid behind the desk. As I scrunched between the desk and the chair, I knocked over a can of pencils. The pencils spilled across the desk, while the can rolled off and clattered to the floor. I grabbed the can and held my breath.

"What was that?" Mr. Henday asked.

"It must be the hamster. She probably knocked over her food again. I'll clean it up, sir."

Silence.

"She's sick and making quite a mess these days."

"Ms. Brewster. In and out. Don't dawdle."

Mr. Henday's silhouette left the door and his footsteps echoed down the hall. The coast was clear. I scooped the pencils into the can. Then I ripped off another strip of tape and ran to Ida's desk. In no time at all, the trap was set.

I opened the door. Trina was avoiding looking at Remi, who was making air hearts frantically. I gave him the thumbs up. He stepped away from the door, just as Eric and the Hoppers rushed into the school. The guys pushed pass Trina and me and entered the classroom.

Remi joined us. "Did you see my signal, Trina? Pretty good, eh?"

She mumbled, "It was okay."

His smiled drooped.

"Great job, Remi," I said. "But you better get back to class. We'll let you know what happens."

He walked down the hall and made one last air heart at Trina, before he rounded the corner. She pretended to look the other way. I felt bad for my friend, knowing how he felt about her and now knowing how she felt about me. I wanted to confess what I had done.

But before I could say anything, Ida ran past me. Her face red from playing tag, she looked out of breath. Trina and I followed her into the class and watched her plop into her seat. I hoped the magnet would be powerful enough to mess with her circuitry. We sat down, looking for any change in Ida. She wiped the sweat from her forehead with her wristband, but otherwise she seemed normal.

The sound of wheels across the tiled floor attracted my attention. Mr. E, wearing an ear-to-ear smile, rolled a sheet-covered cart into the classroom. He paused, while everyone stopped talking and glued their attention to the mystery cart. Once we were all watching, he yanked the sheet off to reveal a collection of batteries, magnets, pencils, light bulbs, wires and small wooden boards. This was a day of experiments; only mine wasn't working. Ida looked perfectly normal.

As Mr. E explained the workings of the electricity experiment, I glanced at Ida. She looked a little pale.

She played with her wristband, then slowly turned and noticed me. She sneered. Our cover was blown. I stared straight ahead at the demonstration.

The lesson seemed to go on forever. Even though I didn't look at her, I could feel Ida glaring at me. It was like she had laser vision and she was burning me from across the class.

"And that's the experiment. Now let's break into science teams," Mr. E said.

Not yet. The magnet needed just a few more seconds to work. I had to keep Ida to stay put for a little longer. I raised my hand.

"I have a question."

"Yes, Marty."

"I don't really understand this electricity thing. If lightning can start fires, how can electricity travel through wires without starting a fire? I don't want to grab the wires and hurt myself."

"You don't have to worry about that. These wires are insulated and the amount of electricity that will go through them is very small. But it's a good question. In general, don't touch wires ever."

"But we're going to touch them now," I said, playing dumb.

Mr. E nodded. "I meant don't touch them unless an expert says the wires are insulated and safe."

"What's insulated mean?" I asked, glancing at Ida, who looked paler.

"What do you think it means?" Mr. E asked.

"I think it means you made fun of someone," I said.

A few of the kids giggled. Eric nodded his head, agreeing with my answer.

"That's *insulted*, Marty. Insul*ated* means it's shielded against the electricity."

"Yeah, dummy," Eric said, pretending he knew what the word meant.

"Eric, we don't use that word in class."

"Sorry."

"Insulated means the electricity can go through the wire without heating the wire. It's made of a material that can take a lot of electricity," Mr. E explained.

"I still don't get it," I said, keeping an eye on Ida, who was positively white. The magnet was working. I had to give it a few more minutes.

"Look at it this way, Marty. You pour water into a paper cone, what happens?"

"The paper will get too wet and water will leak out."

"So what's a better thing to put water in?"

"A glass," I said.

Ida gripped the sides of her desk and tried to stand up.

"Good. A glass is made of material that won't get soaked by the water. The same with insulated wires. They can hold the electricity without getting burned."

"So is electricity like water then?" I asked.

Suddenly, Ida groaned. "Help me."

She swayed back and forth on her feet. The magnet had short-circuited the robot. Suddenly, she collapsed.

"Stay in your seats," Mr. E ordered. "Don't move."

He rushed to his desk and pulled the black pencil case out of his desk drawer. He ran to Ida and gently rolled her on to her side. He opened the case and pulled out a thick pen. He adjusted one end while he lifted Ida's shirt, pinched her stomach and jabbed the pointed end of the pen into her skin.

No one said a thing. No one even breathed. As I watched Mr. E withdraw the pointed end of the pen from Ida's soft tummy, I realized she wasn't made of metal. She was made of flesh. She wasn't a robot. She was human.

FOURTEEN

Eventually colour returned to Ida's face. Her eyes opened and she looked around the room. The kids started to whisper to each other.

"It's okay, Ida. You had a bit of a spell," Mr. E said.

"I'm okay," she said, pushing him away.

"Samantha, please tell the school nurse that I'm bringing Ida to see her."

She nodded and bolted out the door.

"What's wrong with her?" Eric asked.

"It's nothing. Read chapter five in your textbooks."

"I'm fine," Ida said, still struggling to get free of our teacher's hold, but she didn't have much strength. She gave up after a couple of tries.

"We're going to make sure." He lifted Ida to her feet and escorted her out of the classroom, one arm wrapped around her shoulders, holding her up.

As soon as he left, the entire class erupted into chatter. Ten minutes later, Principal Henday arrived and quieted the room. He explained that Ida wasn't feeling well and Mr. E would not return that day.

By lunchtime, everyone in the schoolyard was buzzing about Ida. Even though only the people in the classroom saw her faint, everyone else claimed to know exactly what happened. Some of the girls blamed themselves because they were playing tag with Ida in the morning, while some of the French boys thought Ida was faking it so she could get out of class.

Hannah said, "It was my fault. I tagged her too hard. Daddy says you can get concussions if you're hit too hard."

Samantha sneered. "Hannah, you tagged her on the arm. You have to get hit in the *head* to get concussions."

The French girls had their own theories. Marie argued, "I'll bet it was the flu shots they gave us last week. I bet the nurse had the wrong batch and she gave us something like mad cow disease. So pretty soon we're all going to start passing out."

"Or start mooing," Eric joked.

"I feel kind of faint," Hannah said. "Someone feel my forehead."

The girls stepped back from Hannah and covered their mouths. Marie's flu shot theory sounded like a lot of bull, but I wasn't going to say anything. The best theory came from the most unlikely source. Jacques and Jean Boissonault, the twin bullies, muscled their way through the group.

Jean said, "The same thing happens to our mom sometimes."

Jacques elbowed his brother in the ribs. "Shut up."

Everyone peppered the blond twins with questions. The burly brothers pushed their way out through the crowd, but Jean slowed down and waited until his brother was out of earshot.

Then he turned to us and whispered. "Our mom's got diabetes."

Everyone stopped and looked at each other. No one had any clue what diabetes was. More chatter followed as everyone came up with their own ideas.

"It's a disease where she has to eat bees or else she faints," Eric suggested.

"No, it's like a problem with her legs," a French girl with pigtails chimed in.

"I think she can die from the disease," Samantha declared.

Jean shook his head. "It's not serious. My mom needs to give herself insulin injections every day and she has to be careful about what she eats. Sometimes her levels go off and she faints."

"Ew. Strange," Samantha said.

Eric agreed. "Does it run in the family?"

The other kids stared at Jean to see if he would fall over in front of them.

"It does not," Jean snapped.

Normally, the Boisonnault brothers were the ones who made fun of other kids, but Jean had the same wide-eyed fearful look on his face as his victims. He shuffled away, leaving the kids to guess what else the disease did to people.

Trina whispered in my ear. "I told you Ida wasn't a robot."

"You're right," I said. I'd figured that out when I saw Mr. E stick Ida with the pen, but I wasn't going to say anything, because I was enjoying Trina's lips being so close to my ear.

"We should tell Remi," Trina whispered.

"Follow me." I reluctantly moved away from her sweet lips.

As we headed to the secret meeting place by the school shed to meet Remi, my hand brushed against Trina's arm. A jolt of electricity went up my arm and kicked my heart into a higher gear. I smiled at her, but she looked straight ahead at Remi, who was staring at her from around the corner of the shed. He made another air heart.

When my mom let me have a treat in the store, I always wanted a chocolate bar and a bag of potato chips, but she always told me I had to pick just one. That's how I felt right now. I wanted to keep Remi and Trina as my friends, but I was afraid I might have to pick one over the other.

"Trina, I probably should tell Remi about us on my own."

She nodded.

"We'll meet back here tomorrow," I said.

She veered off to the school fence, trying hard not to look at Remi, who looked back at me and then at her, confused. I jogged up to the shed before he could run after her.

"Where's Trina going?"

"Uh . . . she's not feeling well. She has to go home." I didn't like lying to my friend, but I couldn't tell him the truth just yet.

He started to push past me. "I should walk her home."

"No, she told me the only thing that would make her feel better is if you found her bike." Lying seemed to get easier with each lie I told. Practise made perfect. I felt perfectly sick.

He smiled. "We have to get that bike, and then she'll be so happy she'll tell me that . . . well, you know."

My friend blushed and looked down at his feet.

"Do you really like-*like* Trina that much?" I asked, hoping I could talk him out of liking her.

"Well, yeah."

"What's so great about her anyway?" I asked. "She's got a big mouth."

He grabbed my shirt. "Don't talk about her like that."

As I squirmed away from his grip, I apologized. "I didn't mean anything by it. I just want to make sure you're serious about her."

He let go and smoothed out my shirt. "Sorry. I just want to know how she feels about me. Sometimes, when she accidentally touches my arm, I think she's sending me a secret signal that she like-*likes* me."

I tried to change the subject by explaining what happened to Ida in class and how Mr. E reacted.

"That's weird," he said. "Did Trina think it was weird, too?"

I shrugged. "I don't know, but Mr. E was really worried about Ida."

"Was Trina worried?"

I ignored Remi's question. "I bet he felt bad because he was being so hard on her."

"Is that what Trina thinks?" Remi asked.

I never wanted my friend to shut up before now, but if he was going to ask what Trina thought one more time, I was going to explode.

"The weird thing is that he stayed with her the rest of the day," I said, hoping to get Remi back on track with the investigation.

"Wouldn't they call her parents to get her?"

I shook my head. "Maybe they couldn't come to school right away, so Mr. E had to look after her."

His eyebrows went squiggly like a broken-winged seagull. "Do you know if Mr. E went home?"

"His car's not in the parking lot," I said.

"I think I know why he didn't come back to class. Follow me."

Remi led me to Mr. E's house. His car was parked in front, so we knew he was at home. We settled in across the street for another stake out.

Stakeout Report
By Detectives Boudreau and Chan

4:30   Detective Chan wants me to check out suspect's house. I say it's his turn. Rock, paper, scissors to decide. My rock beats Chan's scissors. Ha!

4:35   Detective Chan says suspect's car is in garage.

4:40   No movement in yard. Trina needs a get-well-soon card.

4:45   I see someone behind curtain of upper floor window. Detective Chan doesn't. I ask him if I should buy Trina flowers. He says she's allergic.

4:52   No more movement in house. How about a Teddy Bear for Trina? Detective Chan says she's allergic. To fake fur?!!!

4:55   Detective Chan wants to chuck a rock against window to get Mr. E to open curtain. My scissors beats his paper. Two in a row for me. Chan tiptoes to house. I think I'll give Trina my Mark Messier hockey card. She's not allergic to paper . . . maybe I should ask. Why is Detective Chan waving at me?

Finally, Remi looked up from the notebook. I pointed to the upper floor window, where Ida was looking out at the street. He smiled as if he knew she'd be there. When she closed the curtains, I ran back to my pal.

"How did you know she'd be here?"

He explained, "If Ida's parents didn't come to school and Mr. E didn't go back to class, that could only mean that Mr. E is Ida's dad."

"Good job," I said. Remi was getting better at this detective work.

"Do you think Trina's going to be impressed?"

"Uh, we still have to find the bike."

He scrunched his face up. He was trying to think of how to get the bike. Finally, he gave up and handed me the notebook. "I guess we're no closer to the bike."

"On the bright side, we know where to find Ida."

"Yeah. Let's call it quits for the day. I have to get home for dinner."

We walked together up the street. He went across the street, while I headed to my parents' store. As I walked, I cracked open the notebook to look over the notes for any clues. When I saw Remi's last entry, my heart jumped up into my throat. How was I going to stop him from making a fool of himself?

FIFTEEN

L ater that night, I slipped my detective's note-book behind the oatmeal raisin cookies that no one ever bought. This secret shelf was where I stored valuables I never wanted my parents to find, including my U.F.O. magazines, secret notes and Eric's video game player. I got this idea, hiding my stuff behind unsold goods, from my dad, who hid his bottle of rye behind the diapers at the back of the store. He didn't want Mom to know he drank. She never found the bottle, which made me think that hiding stuff in the store was a great idea. I pulled the video game out of the hiding place.

Part of me wanted to return the game to Eric, but another part of me realized that I couldn't return it without people suspecting me of stealing. The game was evidence and until I solved the crime, it had to stay hidden.

"Marty," my dad called from the front of the store. "Time to sweep the floor."

I quickly slid the game back and moved the packages of oatmeal raisin cookies in front of the secret stash. Then I headed to the front of the store, where Dad and a broom were waiting for me.

"What were you doing?" he asked.

"Nothing."

Dad shook his head. "If you have nothing to do, it means you're not working hard enough."

Was I his son or his stock boy?

I swept the middle aisle in the store, but I was just moving dirt from one end of the aisle to the other. My mind was somewhere else. I knew I should have told Remi about Trina's feelings about me, but I didn't want to hurt his feelings. I also didn't want Trina to get mad at me. I wasn't looking forward to seeing my two friends the next day. To top it all off, we were nowhere close to catching the thief.

Ida was no robot, but she was the teacher's daughter, which gave her a shield against any kind of accusation. I had to catch her with the stolen goods if I was going to make a case against her.

I crammed the broom under the bread shelf and swept. Out came tiny black flecks that looked like burnt grains of rice. I knew better, though. These weren't grains of rice; they were pieces of mouse poo. Every fall a mouse family would move into my parents' store and every fall my dad would freak out and try to get rid of them.

"Dad, we have mice again," I yelled.

"Aiya!" Dad ran up and surveyed the poo on the floor. "Get the mouse traps."

"Where do we set them?"

"Doesn't matter where. This wouldn't happen if you did a better job of sweeping. From now on, I'm going to watch you do it to make sure it's done right."

"You can trust me, Dad," I said.

"Not if there are mice in the store. I'll put some cheese on and the mice will come to the trap."

"Why cheese?"

"I tried ham and it didn't work. I tried bread and nothing. I think cheese will be the right bait."

Suddenly, the answer to my problems was as obvious as my dad's balding head. The right bait. I might be able to solve the case *and* stop Remi from finding out the truth about Trina and me with the right bait.

The next morning I marched into the schoolyard looking for my detective partners. Remi waited by the school shed. He cradled a box in his hand. I was pretty sure it was the Mark Messier hockey card he was going to give Trina. It looked like he was waiting for the right time to approach her, but she was talking to some kids. Near her, the Lint clung to the side of one of the Hoppers. The kids were gathered around Ida, who glared at everyone, unhappy to be the centre of attention.

"What happened to you?" Trina asked. "We heard you have diabetes."

"No, that's not right. Sometimes I get so nervous I forget to breathe and I black out," Eric said. "Is that what you did?"

"I don't want to talk about it," Ida barked.

"Are you okay now?" Samantha asked. "Or are you still sick?"

A French girl chimed in. "Is diabetes contagious?"

"Duh," said Trina. "She wouldn't come back to school if she was."

"Leave me alone!" Ida yelled. She walked away from the crowd.

Trina spotted me and started to walk over. I tried to wave her off, but she wouldn't stop. Remi jogged from the shed to intercept her. This was going to be a terrible two-person collision, and I was the traffic cop who could prevent the accident. I rushed over to Remi.

"Is that the gift for Trina?" I asked.

He beamed, proudly holding up the black box. "It's my favourite hockey card. Mark Messier, first year on the Oilers."

Remi cracked open the box lid to reveal the hockey card sealed in plastic. A guy in a blue and red Oilers jersey stared ahead at the camera. He looked pretty angry with his big forehead and fierce stare. If this was Remi's hero, I could see why no one ever wanted to play street hockey with him. The card was the bait, and I hoped that I could set the trap without getting my finger caught.

Remi closed the box as Trina came closer. No time to lose. I grabbed the box. "Go along with me. This is going to get her to like-*like* you. Trust me."

"Okay," he said.

She stepped beside us. For a second, there was an awkward silence; none of us knew what to say. Remi looked at me. Trina looked at me. I glanced at the box.

"Remi wanted you to have this," I said.

He smiled. She nodded, but did not return the smile.

"It's okay, Trina," I continued. "I talked to him. He knows everything and he's happy about it."

Her face softened and her smile returned. "I'm so glad you understand, Remi." She touched his arm. He beamed.

"Yes, I understand," he said. Then he whispered in my ear. "Understand what?"

"You'll see," I muttered as I started to walk toward Ida. I walked ahead of Remi and grabbed Trina by the arm. "Follow my lead, okay?"

"Okay, but why?"

"We're going to get your bike back right now," I said.

Remi caught up to us. "What do you need me to do?"

"I want you to give Trina the box in front of Ida and make a big deal about how much it cost."

He stutter-stepped, tripping over his feet. "In front of everyone?"

"Trust me," I said. "Trina, you're going to make a big deal about how much you like it. Got it?"

"In front of everyone?"

"It's part of the plan," I said. "Understand?"

"Totally," she said, then she muttered into my ear. "Understand what?"

Before she could press for an answer, I tossed Remi the box and pushed my two friends toward Ida.

"Wow, I can't believe that you'd give Trina your Mark Messier hockey card," I said loud enough for Ida to hear. The other kids also heard and gathered around us.

I nudged Trina.

"Yes, it's the sweetest thing anyone's ever done for me."

"It's nothing," Remi said.

"How much would something like that cost?" I asked, glancing at Ida.

"About six months allowance," he said, starting to get into my plan. "And I had to return about a hundred empties."

The kids were impressed. "Oooos" came from all around us.

"And you're giving it to Trina?" I prompted him.

"Uh . . . yeah." He handed the box to her.

The kids crowded around her, curious. A lot of the girls were smiling at Remi, while the boys were snickering.

Samantha whispered, "Someone's in love."

Everyone giggled. Remi turned beet red, while Trina's face went white. In the back of the group, Ida stood on her tiptoes to get a closer look at the box. My plan was working.

"I'd keep that hockey card in a safe place," I said. "After Eric's video game went missing, who knows what might happen to stuff like this?"

Finally, Trina clued in to the plan. She cracked a big smile. "Don't worry, Marty. This special gift from Remi is going into my locker. It's going to be completely safe."

"Yeah, no one can break into a locker," I said.

"Thank you so much, Remi," Trina said as she patted his arm. "You're the sweetest."

The girls went "Awwww," while the boys went "Ewwww." Remi's face turned even redder, if that was possible. Even though I knew she was acting, my mouth went dry and my stomach burned like I'd eaten a chili pepper. Trina walked into the school, the girls trailing after her. The boys surrounded Remi and made fun of him, but all he could do was flash a goofy grin. Ida joined the girls following Trina. Would she take the bait?

In class everyone gawked at Trina. Samantha smirked. Hannah giggled. Eric chuckled. Two Hoppers whispered to each other. The Lint asked if they were talking about him or about Trina. Mr. E didn't notice as he described the electricity experiment we were supposed to have done the day before.

While the others were watching Trina, I spied on Ida. If my plan worked, I'd know very quickly.

Sure enough, my prime suspect raised her hand.

"Are you feeling alright?" Mr. E asked. For the first time he didn't sound like he was scolding her.

"I think I have to go to the washroom."

"What's wrong?"

"I have to go, okay? Do you want to know if it's number one or number two?"

Everyone laughed. Mr. E waved at Ida to go. After she left the room, I raised my hand.

"Mr. E, all that talk about going to the washroom makes me have to go, too."

"Why don't you wait until Ida comes back?"

"I don't think I can wait," I said.

"Ew," Trina said. "That fart reeked, Marty."

I didn't really cut the cheese, but Trina was helping me get out of class. Either that, or she was getting even for what I did to her in the schoolyard. Either way, I played along.

"Sorry," I said. "My mom made beans last night."

"Ew. That's so rank I can taste it," Samantha said.

"Oh man, what died inside you?" one of the Hoppers asked.

"Yeah, what died inside you?" The Lint echoed the Hopper.

I was amazed at the power of Trina's suggestion. She could make people smell a fart that never even existed. Even *I* could smell something bad. Another tiny pop of air came from Trina's direction. She flashed me a sheepish grin. She wasn't using the power of suggestion.

"Ew," she cried. "Mr. E, make him go away."

"Okay, okay, Marty. Go to the bathroom."

"Thanks." I dashed out.

I headed down the hallway in the direction opposite to the bathrooms. I moved silently in case Ida had sensitive ears. As I reached the hallway intersection I peeked around the corner. Ida knelt in front of Trina's locker. She pulled something black from her cotton wristband and stuck it in the combination lock. She started to jiggle the thing in the lock. I crept up behind her, close enough to see that what she'd been sticking into the lock was the sharpened end of a hairpin. The lock sprang open. I crept toward her, but my sneakers squeaked on the waxed floor.

Ida spun around, holding Remi's hockey card box. "What are you doing here?"

"Gotcha," I said. "I caught you red-handed with the stolen goods."

"It's your word against mine. And no one's going to believe you after they find out you stole Eric's video game."

So, *she* had planted the game. "You were trying to frame me."

"I don't know what you're talking about," she said, batting her eyes at me.

She stood up and started to walk away. I grabbed her arm, wrapping my hand around her wristband. I could feel something under it. Ida tried to pull away, but I hung on tight.

"Be careful, or I might have to tell your girlfriend what kind of boy you are," Ida said.

"I don't have a girlfriend."

"'M.C. plus T.B.' That's so sweet. You're in love." How had she cracked the code on my green scribbler?

"You stole my scribbler," I accused.

"What *ever* are you talking about? I'm innocent." Ida batted her eyes. "Now let go or I'll have to tell your French friend about you and Trina. I don't think he'll be too happy to hear that. He looked like he was pretty much in love with her when he gave her his precious hockey card."

She pulled her arm away, but the cotton wristband slipped off, uncovering a metal bracelet with an ID tag. She covered the rectangular tag and walked toward the class. I wasn't going to let her go that easily.

"I don't think your dad will be too happy to know you're trying to get rid of the bracelet," I said. There was something important about that bracelet, but I didn't know what. Until I learned what it really was, I had to bluff. "That's right. I know Mr. E is your dad."

"Smooth move, Sherlock. Any dum-dum could have figured that out."

I wasn't going to let her throw me off my game. "I know he wants you to wear that bracelet, and I'll bet he'd be pretty upset if he knew you were trying to get rid of it."

"How would you like a Medi-bracelet that reminds you that you're sick?"

"What's so bad about that?"

"People see this and they think I'm just a poor little sick girl. You don't know what it's like."

But I did. Being Chinese, I knew exactly what it was like to be judged for something I had no control over. She could take off her bracelet any time. I couldn't change the way I looked or who I was.

"You can take it off," I said.

She squirmed for a second. "I can't."

"Why not? Is it because you're afraid of what your dad will do?"

She shook her head. "I need to wear it for when he isn't around."

As much as she hated the thing, she knew she needed it, which probably made her hate it even more. She was caught between two opposites, just like I was torn between my friendship with Remi and my feelings toward Trina.

"It's not a big deal," I said.

"Leave me alone," she snapped at me. "I wish I never came here. I don't want to be Diab-Ida again. Take this stupid thing. I don't need it any more."

She threw the hockey card box at me. It bounced off my chest. I fumbled for it and barely caught it. When I looked up, I saw Mr. E looking right at us.

"I caught Marty trying to break into a locker." Ida pointed at me. "He's the one who's been stealing. He's got the loot in his hands."

"Is that yours, Marty?" my teacher asked.

Slowly, I shook my head. Ida had framed me.

Sixteen

Sitting in Principal Henday's office was like sitting in a dentist's chair waiting for the dentist to drive the dental probe under my gums and dig for plaque. I imagined all the terrible things that might happen to me, and the longer I waited, the more terrible things I thought. I wondered if Mr. Henday earned his nickname, the Rake, not for being tall and skinny, but for using a rake to punish bad kids. Maybe he'd give me a hundred days' detention. No, worse, he would make me clean the bathrooms with a toothbrush. Or worst of all, he'd call the police and I'd have to go to jail for a crime I didn't commit. But as bad as the things were that I thought he'd do, nothing compared to what he actually did.

"Mr. Chan," he said. "I'm going to have to talk to your father about this."

If Dad found out I'd made any kind of trouble at school, he'd hit the roof. "I didn't steal anything, Mr. Henday," I argued.

"Don't make this any worse for yourself. Come clean, Mr. Chan. Confession is good for the soul."

Confession was only good if I admitted to what the Rake thought I'd done. If I told him the truth, he'd say I was lying. The problem with grown-ups was that they only wanted to hear what they *wanted* me to say. I knew I wasn't going to convince anyone about the truth, so I just stared at my lap and waited for Mr. Henday to yell at me.

"What do you have to say for yourself?" he barked.

Accusing the teacher's daughter of being a thief would be like sticking my tongue on an icy fence post. I decided to keep my tongue in my mouth and save myself the pain.

"Last chance, Mr. Chan," he said.

I looked up and said nothing. Mr. Henday folded his arms across his chest, his Finger of Confession poised to tap against his elbow.

"You're not going to believe me anyway," I said.

The Rake tapped his elbow once. "I'm waiting."

Tap. Tap. *Tap. Tap. Tap. Tap. Tap. Tap. Tap. Tap.*

Instead of staring at his finger, I stared right into my principal's eyes. "I did nothing wrong."

The tapping stopped. Mr. Henday unfolded his arms and reached for the telephone. "I want you to know that I don't like doing this, Mr. Chan."

He dialled and placed the receiver to his ear. The curly phone cord reminded me of a hangman's noose. "Mr. Chan, yes, this is Principal Henday calling. We need to talk about your son. Do you have time to come down to the school? Yes, I understand you're running a business. I wouldn't have called if this matter weren't absolutely urgent. Again, I'm sorry to take you away from the store, but I must insist you come to the school. Your son has been accused of stealing."

Mr. Henday jerked the receiver away from his ear. My Dad's voice was loud enough for me to hear even without the telephone. It was probably loud enough for the secretary in the next room to hear. Mr. Henday spoke again.

"I'll see you in a few minutes, Mr. Chan."

The Rake hung up the phone. The sound of the receiver hitting the cradle made me think of the chop of an executioner's axe.

Dad never visited the school. *Ever.* He never came to school concerts or Christmas shows or track and field meets. He never took me to class. He never picked me up. I was surprised he even knew where the school was. I think he was ashamed to come to my school, because he'd dropped out of school in China. But now Dad was not only in a school, he was in the Rake's office, and I was the one responsible for making him sit in the principal's office.

"My son will not steal again," Dad said, his anger vein bulging in the middle of his forehead.

The growing vein meant that he was incredibly mad, but couldn't blow off steam because he was around people. The bigger the vein grew, the madder dad was. Right now, the vein looked gigantic.

"But I didn't steal anything," I argued.

"Quiet," Dad said through gritted teeth.

"Mr. Chan," Mr. Henday said.

Both Dad and I looked at Mr. Henday and said "Yes?"

"I meant your father."

I looked down at my lap.

"Mr. Chan, I know this is going to be difficult, but I'm going to have to ask you to search your home for a bicycle and a video game. Marty may have hidden them somewhere."

For a few minutes, no one said a thing. I felt like time had stopped and the only way it would move forward was to look up, but I had a pretty good idea what was going to happen to me when time moved again. I stared at my lap, trying to keep time from moving.

Dad kick-started time and my chair. "We're going home now."

I didn't budge, hoping that time could stop again.

"Now!"

There was no way Dad was going to listen to any kind of explanation. The Vein was controlling him and The Vein was saying "Get out of the office and yell at your son." On the way home, Dad obeyed The Vein's instructions to the letter.

By the time we got back to the store the vein had returned to normal size, but Dad was still pretty mad. He and Mom turned over everything in my bedroom. They didn't find Eric's game or the bicycle, but they weren't going to stop with just my bedroom.

"Maybe he hide it in the store," Mom suggested.

"His principal said there was a video game."

They started to head out of my room. If they looked behind the oatmeal raisin cookies, I was done for. I had to stop the search.

"I didn't take anything, Mom. You can look in the store. Start with the diapers. You won't find anything."

Dad slowed down. Mom bumped into him.

"You don't want to look behind the diapers," I said.

Dad turned around. "You know what? I don't think he hid anything in the store. Our customers would have found it by now. Keep looking in his room."

They turned over my mattress where I kept the oven mitts I used as hockey gloves.

"Aiya," Mom said. "You steal these."

"No, Mom, I was just using them."

"Why you need them?" she asked.

"Hockey gloves."

"It's his friend. He make Marty do this," Dad said.

I shook my head.

"You always let him come in the store," Mom accused Dad.

"That boy isn't allowed here ever again," he yelled. "And you have to watch your son more carefully."

Even though they were mad at me, they seemed to take it out on each other. I hated hearing them yell at each other. It was worse than listening to fingernails across a blackboard. When they'd finished searching

167

my room, Mom sat me down in the butcher area of the store while Dad paced behind her.

"No more taking things from the store," she said.

I nodded. "I'm sorry."

"Make him tell you where he hid the things he stole," Dad ordered. He was so mad he could only talk to me through Mom.

"Marty, you tell your dad what you do with the bike and the game."

I said nothing. Dad was a raging wildfire and anything I said would just be more kindling for the blaze.

"Tell him he is grounded until he shows us where he put the things," Dad barked.

"You are grounded," Mom said.

Dad continued to yell at Mom to yell at me, while she repeated everything he said. Eventually, Dad was yelled out. He told her to tell me to go work in the store. My punishment wasn't very different from what I had to do on a normal school day. The only difference was that Dad used every chance he could to tell me that stealing was bad.

As I stood on a pop crate to ring in groceries on the cash register, Dad talked to the customers about what I had done. Mrs. Johnson, the oldest driver in the world, piled her groceries on to the counter while Dad tried to teach me a lesson through her.

"Mrs. Johnson, tell my son that stealing is bad."

"Excuse me?" Mrs. Johnson said, turning up her hearing aid.

"My son doesn't understand that stealing is a bad thing," he said.

I punched in the groceries, trying not to make eye contact with the grey-haired Mrs. Johnson.

"Marty, stealing hurts everyone," Dad said. "You take from people, you not only take away their things, but you also take away their feelings that people are good."

"I didn't steal," I mumbled.

"Mrs. Johnson, you agree with me, right?"

She placed a couple of cans on the counter. "Well, that's the last of it," she said, ignoring Dad's question.

"Stealing is the worst thing anyone could do to someone else. Maybe my son thinks it's a little thing that was taken, but big or small, it doesn't matter. If you steal, it's wrong, and someone will catch you sooner or later."

I rang in the last of the groceries. "Mrs. Johnson, will that be all?"

She sheepishly looked at my dad and whispered, "I ate some grapes while I was shopping. Please charge me for them."

"I wasn't talking about you, Mrs. Johnson," Dad tried to explain.

I wanted to crawl into the cash register and slam the drawer shut. As long as Ida stuck to her story, I'd never be able to clear my name. I had to bring her to justice. To do that, I needed to prove that Ida was the thief.

SEVENTEEN

The next day, the kids at school treated me differently. Samantha clutched her backpack to her chest when I came near. Other kids steered clear of me and checked their pockets after I walked past them. There was a saying that a person was innocent until proven guilty, but this was a lie that people said to make the accused feel better. In the court of schoolyard opinion, this saying held as much water as Mom telling me that watching too much TV would make my eyes turn square. In the real world my eyes didn't turn square and in the schoolyard the kids only needed to hear Ida's accusation to believe I was a thief.

Eric Johnson charged across the field toward me. He moved like an oncoming car and I was a doe caught in the headlights of his angry eyes. He grabbed me by the shirt and nearly lifted me off my feet.

"Give me my game," he shouted.

"I didn't take it," I explained.

He cocked his fist back. I scanned the schoolyard for help, but everyone was cheering Eric on. He swung at me but didn't connect. Remi grabbed Eric from behind. Remi grunted. "Say you're sorry."

Eric struggled for a second, but couldn't break out of my friend's iron clinch. "No."

"Say it."

Eric's shoulders sagged. "Sorry."

Remi let go. Eric shuffled away, glaring at me. Even though he didn't say another word, I knew what he was thinking from the scowl across his red face. Around me the kids pointed and muttered to each other, but no one said anything aloud. Remi grabbed me and pulled me away.

"Thanks, Remi," I said, as we walked away.

"No problem," he said. "But I don't think anyone's going to invite you to their house."

I nodded. "That's okay as long as you will."

"I have to count the spoons first," Remi joked.

I chuckled. I was so glad that Remi was my friend, because he always knew the right thing to say.

"So what do we do to clear your name?"

"We have to get Ida to confess," I said. "Where is she?"

He pointed across the schoolyard. Ida, grinning at us, leaned against the granite statue of Jesus. I marched toward her with my friend on my heels. Ida stepped away from the statue, adjusted her wristband, and met us halfway across the field.

"You're not getting away with this," I told her.

Remi backed me up. "We're on to you." He squinted at her. Apparently, he remembered my mother's squint-errogation technique.

"You guys can't pin anything on me. In fact, I wouldn't be surprised if Trina's bike showed up behind your dad's store."

Blackmail was an ugly game, but I wasn't going to let Ida win. I wished I had my dad's tape recorder to capture her confession, but I wasn't allowed to use it after the Graffiti Ghoul case.

"Why are you doing this?" I asked. "We didn't do anything to you."

"I've been watching you and your girlfriend spy on me in class, and I don't like it."

Remi's eyebrows arched up.

"She's not my girlfriend," I said, looking at Remi.

Her eyes widened as she guessed the truth. "He doesn't know, does he? Do you want to know a secret, Frenchie? Your friend here — "

I cut her off. "You are going to admit what you did," I said. "Or else."

"Or else what? I can tell your friend everything."

"What's she talking about?" Remi asked.

"We have proof you took everything, Ida." I had to stop her from blurting what she saw in my secret green scribbler, even if it meant bluffing.

"Who are people going to believe? Me or a bunch of nosy hyenas with a notebook?"

The pieces started to fall together. The reason why she broke into my locker was to get my detective's notebook, but I never left it in my locker. I always kept it close to me. She grabbed my secret scribbler, mistaking it for the detective notebook, and that's how she discovered my real feelings for Trina. The feelings I had hidden in the back of the scribbler, and now had to hide from my best friend.

"Face it, Marty, I have a lot of secrets I can tell. And they'd hurt you way more than they'd hurt me."

She knew she had me.

Remi leaned in. "What do you know?"

"Things," she said, looking right at me.

"Just because you're the teacher's daughter, you think you can get away with anything," I said.

"It's exactly the opposite," she said, glaring.

He jumped in. "No way. The nutty professor will let you get away with anything."

"Don't call my dad that," she snapped.

"You mean the mad science teacher?" Remi asked.

"Shut up. He's not mad."

Ida was sending mixed signals. She hated her dad, but she also protected him. How did she really feel about her father?

"He's a maniac."

Ida wound up to slap Remi, but I grabbed her wrist. I felt the Medi-bracelet under the cotton material. She pulled her arm away.

"You think I don't know he's embarrassing? I don't need any more reminders. Especially not from snoops like you."

Sometimes I felt the same way she did. My parents were so embarrassing I wished I was adopted. Sometimes I wished I could choose new parents. I never thought a teacher's daughter would feel the same way. I figured being related to a teacher was like having a get-out-of-jail-free card.

Ida stomped away. Remi started after her, but I stopped him.

"Why are we letting her go?"

"Give her time to stew. She'll start to panic soon enough and then she'll slip up."

"What secrets was she talking about, Marty?"

"She was bluffing," I lied. She knew the very thing I needed to keep secret.

As Ida crossed the schoolyard, Mr. E intercepted her. I couldn't make out what he was saying to her. She ripped off her cotton wristband and threw it at him. He pointed in the direction of the school, and she obeyed. She covered her Medi-bracelet with her other hand as she ran into the building.

He put the wristband in his pocket. He was trying to control Ida, just like my dad was trying to control me, but the more he tried to keep her under control, the more she wanted to act out. Then the truth splashed across my face like a jet of fountain water.

Ida hated Mr. E because he only saw her as his diabetic daughter. The final piece of the puzzle fell into place. I finally knew why she stole. She wanted to be known for being something *other* than the sick girl.

When I told Remi this, he shook his head. "Why wouldn't she say she was the thief then? Why hide from it now?"

"Remember when we talked about what we wanted to do to the Boissonault brothers to teach them for bullying everyone?"

"Like make them lick the bottom of my shoe after I visited my uncle's pig farm?"

I nodded. "But when they came around, we didn't do a thing. Why is that?"

He shrugged. "Because I like keeping all my teeth."

"Exactly. Ida might want to get caught, but she chickens out when it's time to take the blame."

"That's why she's taunting us. She wants us to catch her."

"Exactly," I said. "And I know just how to do it."

Eighteen

In Mr. E's class, I tried to talk to Trina, but she wouldn't even look at me. Every time I tapped her on the shoulder, she shrugged me off like I was a pesky mosquito. When I tried to drop a note over her shoulder, she let it fall to the floor without even looking down. Instead, she stared straight ahead at Mr. E. Was she afraid of getting me into more trouble?

Finally, I leaned toward the back of her head and whispered, "We need to talk."

She leaned back and muttered, "Why is Remi still acting as if he like-*likes* me?"

Had she figured out the truth? My bait trap had caught only one person: me. Trina turned around. I didn't want to lose her, but I knew if she didn't get a good answer, she'd come up with her own.

"It's still part of the plan," I whispered.

Mr. E barked without turning around. "I hear a lot of chatter but not a lot of writing."

Trina leaned forward and copied down the notes that our teacher was writing on the whiteboard. I waited for a few minutes. Eric started to shuffle around in his desk. Near the front, a few of the girls started chattering with each other. The Lint was offering one of the Hoppers a melted chocolate bar from his front pocket. The classroom noise was building enough to give me cover. I tapped Trina on the shoulder. She leaned back.

I whispered, "You have to keep pretending so that Ida thinks you don't care about me. The plan's on the note."

She didn't look back, but she nodded. Then she pretended to scratch her left foot. She picked up the note and read it. Once she was done, she crumpled the note and stuck it in her mouth and ate it.

On Saturday the first phase of the plan went into action. I pulled Eric's stolen video game from its secret cookie hiding place and slipped it into my backpack. As I did I noticed, a few feet over, a rye bottle behind packages of unsalted crackers. Dad had moved his hiding place. I made a note to move my hiding spot when I came back. I replaced the cookie package and hid my backpack in the storeroom at the back of the store.

Phase one was easy. Phase two would be much harder. I had to get out of the building. I found dad behind the cash register.

"Dad, can I go out and play?" I asked.

"No, you're grounded and we're busy."

There wasn't a single customer in the entire store, just like every Saturday morning.

"No one's here," I said.

"Then you have plenty of time to mop the floor before the customers come."

Mom rolled the mop bucket out, using the mop handle as a rudder. "Start behind the meat counter."

"Mom, can't I go out for a little while? I've been good all week."

She shook her head. "What your dad say is what you do."

Mom lied. I was pretty sure that what *she* said was the golden rule. She only pretended to let dad make the law. I had to convince her that it was a good idea to let me out. I pulled the mop out and swished the wet head under the wooden butcher's block.

"Mom, there's so much garbage here. The flies are going to get to it. Do you want me to take it out?"

She nodded. I grabbed two bulging black bags and lugged them to the back of the store. I grabbed my backpack and headed outside, where Trina waited for me.

"Took you long enough," she said.

"You don't know my parents."

"Well, you'd better hurry. Remi's watching Mr. E's house. He saw Mr. E drive away. We might not have much time."

We ran to Mr. E's house. I had to go slow to keep from banging up the video game in my backpack. We spotted Remi outside the hedge of Mr. E's red brick Asylum House.

"Was Ida with Mr. E?" I asked.

He shrugged. "Not sure. I saw the car pull away, but there's been no movement in the yard or the house for an hour. I'm surprised you got out of the store that fast."

Trina cocked her head and looked at him, puzzled. He knew my parents all too well. I pulled out the video game.

"Okay, we plant the evidence in the yard so Mr. E can find it," I said. "Then we phone in an anonymous tip. If he's anything like my dad, once he finds the game, he'll look for anything else Ida might have taken. Chances are he'll find your bike."

Trina nodded. Remi gave the thumbs up.

We headed to the gate. I peeked through the slats. No sign of movement. The coast was clear. Trina pulled open the gate and I slipped into the junkyard. What I saw stopped me in my tracks.

In the middle of the yard, the Ida robot was no longer on top of the table. Gone was her buzz saw hand. Instead both her arms were croquet mallets. Her torso was mounted on what looked like a wagon that had tank-like treads. This robot could do some serious damage.

"Wow!" Remi exclaimed.

"It looks so creepy with Ida's head on top," Trina said.

We kept our distance from the robot as we headed to the house.

"Let's plant the game in a place that's easy to find, but not out in the open. It has to look like Ida was trying to hide her loot."

"Under the stairs," Trina suggested.

"Good idea, Trina," Remi said. "I was going to say that too. I guess great minds think alike, eh?"

She didn't answer him. Instead, she knelt in front of the wooden steps and peeked under. She held out her hand to grab the video game from me, but before I could pass it to her, a giant whirring noise filled the air.

Behind us, the Ida robot had come to life and her mallet arms were swinging.

Nineteen

The robot lurched forward. I pushed Trina and Remi to either side of the porch and backed up the wooden steps. The Ida robot moved to the edge of the steps, while I backed up to the door of the porch. The mallet arms bashed the porch landing, but I was in no danger.

"Get out of the yard," I yelled at Remi and Trina.

But they weren't going to leave me. He picked up a pipe; she grabbed a trashcan lid. They advanced on the Ida robot. The machine must have sensed the attack, because it veered backward and spun around to face Trina. She backed up as the robot's mallet arms clanged against her trashcan-lid shield. Trina slipped on a refrigerator door and lost her balance. The robot surged ahead, its arms swinging away.

"Save Trina," I ordered Remi as I jumped off the porch.

The Mystery of the Mad Science Teacher

I scooped up a pipe from the mess on the lawn, just as he ran in front of the Ida Robot and blocked the swinging mallet with his pipe. Trina scrambled to her feet and blocked the other mallet with her silver shield.

I crept behind the robot, hoping to find a weak spot. Remembering the circuit boards in the machine's body, I speared the pipe at the Ida robot's back. I hoped to mess up the internal circuits, but my pipe glanced off the armour.

"Get Trina out of there!" I yelled.

"I can take care of myself," Trina yelled back.

Suddenly, the Ida head spun around and looked right at me with its glowing red eyes. The robot spoke, but the lips did not move in sync.

"Nice try, Marty," the voice said. It sounded like Ida's voice coming through the robot's speaker system. "But I caught you trespassing on my property. You're criminals."

The robot's treads rolled over a green refrigerator door and gained traction on the brown lawn as it herded Remi and Trina toward the fence. I chased after it and speared the robot's back. The Ida head shook side to side as if it were mocking me. As we got to the edge of the fence, the robot stopped. The arms lowered.

"You did it!" Trina yelled from behind her trashcan lid.

Remi lowered his pipe and gave me a thumbs-up sign. I didn't know what I did.

"Stupid controller!" yelled Ida from behind. She now stood on the porch, holding a radio controller. She pushed a button and pointed the black box at the robot, which sparked back to life and swung at my friends. They blocked the blows and tried to get out of the path of the rolling robot.

I continued to spear the robot, but I was doing no damage as Ida's laughter boomed out of the robot's speaker. I lowered my guard, and the robot body swivelled around to face me. One of the mallet arms came down at my head. I held up my pipe just in the nick of time and had to back up as the robot advanced on me.

Behind the robot, Remi swung at the machine's head, while Trina scrambled over the junk pile to the far end of the yard. Too late, we realized that this switch in direction was part of a trap. The robot backed me inside a doorless refrigerator and blocked off any escape.

Then the robot started rocking the refrigerator back and forth. I think it was trying to tip the thing over on its front so I'd be trapped inside.

"Get me out of here, Remi!"

"I'm working on it!" my friend screamed back as he swung at the robot. I could barely see him, but every now and then I saw the pipe smack against the robot's head. One blow knocked its wig to one side and revealed the metal skull underneath. One eye flickered and winked out.

The robot spun around and chased Remi. He tripped over a car engine and lost his pipe. As he tried to scramble back to his feet, I climbed out of the refrigerator, but I couldn't reach my friend. The Ida robot swung its mallet arms at him.

Clang, clang!

Trina jumped in front of Remi with her trashcan shield and deflected the blows.

"Get up, Remi!" She screamed.

"I can't. I twisted my ankle," he said.

"Then crawl!" I shouted.

He scrambled across the junkyard while Trina covered him. The robot advanced. I tried swinging my pipe against its head and I knocked off the wig. The Ida head looked like a cyborg from a horror movie. The one working red eye gleamed at me as the machine rolled at my friends.

The clatter of the wooden mallets against Trina's shield was so loud I wondered why no neighbours had come to check on the noise. I yelled for help, but I could barely hear my own voice above the clang of the battle.

Finally Remi and Trina had nowhere else to go. They were cornered. The robot blocked off any escape with its swinging mallet arms.

"You're going to be sorry you ever tried to take me on," Ida said from the porch.

She pushed another button and the Ida robot inched closer to my friends. Enough was enough. I tossed my pipe at the robot, but it clanged off the metal body and fell uselessly to the ground. I sprinted across the obstacle course of junk toward the human Ida.

"Stay back or else," she threatened.

Ignoring her threat, I jumped up the stairs two at a time.

"I push this button and the Ida robot runs right over your friends."

"You're not hurting anyone."

I advanced on her. The porch creaked under my steps. In the yard, the robot continued to batter Trina's shield. The clang of mallets against metal filled the yard.

"You can't save your girlfriend," Ida yelled.

"Shut up!" I grabbed the controller.

As Ida and I wrestled for the controller, the robot went out of control. It veered away from Remi and Trina, and then charged at them. The arms spun like a windmill as the robot pivoted around the yard, smashing into the scrap metal, knocking over the refrigerator and then skidding to a stop and moving in a new direction.

Trina helped Remi to his feet and the two of them flattened themselves against the hedge to avoid getting run over.

"Let go!" Ida yelled.

My fingers fumbled over the levers on the controller. My thumb caught against a lever, which must have controlled the robot's direction, because the metal wrecking machine came straight for the porch. Just as the robot smashed into the porch I pulled Ida out of the way. I could hear wood cracking — the robot busted through the porch's wooden lattice. I let her have the controller. She tried to back the robot out, but it was wedged under the porch. The treads spun, kicking up dirt and grass, then finally stopped. It was stuck.

"You've lost, Ida," I said. "You might as well give up."

"You're not the boss of me," she said. Then she called across the yard, "Do you really want to help this guy after what he did to you, Remi?"

"Don't listen to her," I said.

"He has a crush on Trina," she said.

Remi hobbled forward. "No, he doesn't."

"I have a little scribbler that says different."

Trina stepped forward. "Marty, you said you told Remi and he was okay about us."

He looked at her, eyes wide with shock. "Do you like Marty?"

She said nothing, but her silence was as good as a yes.

Ida cackled. "Oh, this is great. I thought it was just a secret crush, but it's more than that. How do you feel now, Remi?"

She waved the controller in front of me, taunting me. The real Ida was doing more damage than the robot Ida ever could.

"Why didn't you tell him?" Trina said, scolding me.

"I told you how I felt about her," Remi said. "You knew I liked her and you still did this — "

"I can explain."

Ida laughed. "Poor Remi. After you gave your precious hockey card to Trina in front of everyone in the school. And now you find out she likes your best friend. Ouch."

"You lied to me," he accused me.

I walked toward him. "I didn't want to hurt your feelings."

"You said you told him everything," Trina said, glaring at me. "You lied to me, too."

"I'm sorry," I mumbled.

Neither of my friends would even look at me.

"Let's go, Remi," Trina said.

She tried to help him out of the yard, but he waved her away.

"I still like you as a friend, Remi," she said.

He limped away.

"Some friend you are," Ida said to me, sneering.

Ignoring her taunt, I ran off the porch and intercepted Remi. He wouldn't look at me, but Trina shot her laser beam glare through my sweaty forehead.

"I was trying to protect you guys," I said to them both, looking from Trina to Remi, hoping one of them would understand. "It was for your own good."

"Liar," Ida said. "You were trying to protect yourself. You're a selfish jerk."

"I didn't want anyone to get hurt," I yelled back.

She came to the steps. "You didn't care about anyone other than yourself."

Remi said nothing. Trina didn't have to. Ida was saying exactly what they were thinking.

She continued, "You never once thought about them. You kept them in the dark because you thought you knew better. You wouldn't let them decide anything for themselves. You were so busy trying to protect them from the truth, you hurt them even more. You're exactly like my dad."

She was right. I had become just like Mr. E and my dad. Instead of thinking about Remi and Trina first, I thought about me. How could I have done this to my friends?

"Is that what you really think, Ida?" Mr. E said.

I turned around. Our teacher stood at the gate. I don't know when he showed up, but I guessed he'd heard enough to know that Ida's speech wasn't for me; it was for him. On the porch, Ida stared right at her dad. Her eyes looked wet with tears, but she kept her hands at her sides.

Mr. E walked across the yard and examined the damage done by the Ida robot. While most of the scrap metal could be moved, I don't think Mr. E could overlook the fact that the robot had smashed through the porch.

"My daughter never has friends over," he said. "Now I can see why."

Remi looked down. Trina said nothing. I looked up at Mr. E, hoping he was joking. He wasn't smiling.

Ida yelled, "They broke into the yard! I was trying to defend the house."

"Why would these kids break into our yard?"

"They stole the video game. They were trying to frame me." She pointed at the video game by her feet.

Mr. E shushed her with a finger to his lips. He turned to us. "Mr. Chan, I seem to remember my daughter caught you stealing at school. Do you deny that?"

I said nothing.

"And now you've dragged your accomplices into this crime," he said.

Remi and Trina looked up, their eyes wide with fear.

I shook my head. "No, they're not accomplices, sir. They were trying to save me. They had nothing to do with this."

I confessed to a crime I didn't commit so I could save my friends. Remi looked up at me, shocked. Trina shook her head, signalling me to keep quiet.

"I'm the one behind it all," I said.

"Vandalism and trespassing is serious business, Mr. Chan. I may have to call your parents. Perhaps even the police."

I looked at Ida. She crossed her arms, holding the controller. She glared back at me. Was she upset I was taking away her credit again, or was she scared of getting in trouble?

"Should we call the police, Ida?" Mr. E asked.

"I don't care," she mumbled.

Trina shook her head. "She tried to run us over with the robot. She's the one who's started all of this. She stole my bike."

Mr. E motioned Trina to come closer. "Why do you think my daughter did this, Ms. Brewster?"

"Because she's a thief," Remi piped up.

"If she is a thief, does that give you three the right to come into my yard and destroy my equipment?"

No one spoke.

"My Ida robot may not look like much, but it took a lot of time and energy for Ida and me to build this machine."

"No, no, no! I'm sick of hearing about that stupid robot," Ida yelled. "We didn't build it together. You did it by yourself."

"Don't take that tone with me, Ida," Mr. E warned.

"All you care about is your stupid robot. You spend more time with it than with me. The only time you ever spend with me is when it's time for my tests and shots."

"I want you to get better."

"Dad, I have to take these stupid insulin shots for the rest of my life. That's not getting better. That's a prison sentence. And playing with robots isn't going to make me feel better about anything."

"You used to like robots. You were my budding scientist," he said.

"I hate robots. I hate science. I hate it all," Ida yelled. She lifted the controller and flipped one of the levers. The robot roared to life and started to spin its treads against the lawn, kicking up dirt and grass.

"Ida, stop it! What are you doing?"

"I'm driving this stupid thing into traffic and I hope Mrs. Johnson comes by with her Cadillac and runs it over!"

Remi, Trina and I took a few steps back as the Ida robot tore free of the porch. It dragged part of the wooden lattice with it as it backed up.

Hooked to the front of the machine was Trina's bicycle.

Ida let go of the lever. The robot powered down. Mr. E looked at the bike and then at his daughter. She glared at me for a few seconds.

"Yes, I did it," she yelled. "You happy, Dad? I'm not Diab-Ida any more. I'm the girl who steals. What do you think of that?! Do you even care?"

She broke down in tears. She dropped the controller and sobbed. Mr. E walked over and hugged his daughter.

"It's okay, Ida. We'll work through this."

Mr. E wasn't the mad science teacher any more. He looked more like the sad science teacher. If I had done what Ida did, I'm pretty sure my dad would not have hugged me.

Remi nudged me in the ribs and whispered, "Just because you tried to be the hero back there doesn't mean you're in the clear for lying to me. You're playing net for the next seventeen game-seven finals."

He smiled. My lie wasn't sharp enough to cut the bonds of our friendship.

I only hoped Trina would be so quick to forgive me.

"I'm sorry," I whispered to her.

She looked at me, her eyes welling up. Then she wound up and punched me in the gut. "Not as sorry as you're going to be," she said as she walked over to the porch to check on her bike.

Over the next week, Mr. E told everyone what really happened, clearing my name with Principal Henday and making sure that the kids didn't treat me like a criminal. He even tried to talk to my parents, but Dad was still mad at me for skipping out on my chores. Mr. E had suggested a good punishment. Even though our teacher knew that Ida was responsible for stealing the bike, he still said we were responsible for destroying his robot and his yard. Trina, Remi and I had to help Ida every weekend to rebuild his porch, clean up the yard and fix the Ida robot. Dad agreed to let me do this, but only after I finished the chores at the store.

While we worked in the yard, I tried to patch things up with Trina. She hadn't talked to me for three weeks, even though I started every conversation with "I'm really, really, really sorry." I hoped the more "really's" I added before sorry would soften her heart. I was trying so hard to win her over I started to feel like The Lint with the Hoppers.

Finally one Sunday, after we'd finished patching up the last of the lattice and cleared most of the junk from the yard, Trina walked over.

"Did I say I was sorry?" I said.

"About a million times," she said.

"Well, I *am* really, really, really, really sorry."

She bit her lip for a second, making me wait. Then she playfully punched my arm.

"Ow," I said.

"Serves you right, Chan," Remi said, grinning.

Ida rolled her eyes at us.

"We could all start over as friends," Trina said, looking at Ida and me. I wasn't sure which one of us she was talking to, until she held out her hand for me to shake it.

Ida rolled her eyes again as I shook Trina's hand.

Remi clapped his arms around the two of us. "I think there's a street hockey game calling us. Ida, you want to play?"

She shrugged. "Whatever." The way she said "whatever" made me think she wasn't too miffed about the invitation.

"I'll play forward," Trina said.

"That leaves you in goal," he said, pointing at me.

I groaned, but I only half meant it. I could put up with a few stinging pucks as long as it meant I was keeping a promise to a friend.

MARTY CHAN is a nationally-known dramatist, screenwriter and author. He is a former Gemini-nominated and gold medal winner for "The Orange Seed Myth and Other Lies Mothers Tell", and the winner of the 2005 Edmonton Book Prize for his first novel in the Chan Mystery Series, *The Mystery of the Frozen Brains.* The second in the Series, *The Mystery of the Graffiti Ghoul,* was shortlisted for three 2007 young readers' choice awards and the 2007 Arthur Ellis Crime Writers of Canada Award in the Best Juvenile category. Marty Chan lives in Edmonton, Alberta.

CPSIA information can be obtained
at www.ICGtesting.com
Printed in the USA
LVHW01s0445151117
556321LV00001B/1/P